DITCH OF THE DAMNED

AND OTHER TALES

RYAN HOYT

MACHETE & QUILL PRESS

Paperback ISBN: 978-1-956163-15-5

Ebook ISBN: 978-1-956163-16-2

DITCH OF THE DAMNED

AND OTHER TALES

Contents

Introduction

This is a short collection. While I focus most of my writing efforts on novel-length stories, I sometimes get inspiration for a story that can only be told in a short enough form to be impactful. I included a preface for each story that will give you some insight into my intent with the story or how the concept came to me.

Most of my horror work is set in the fictional town of Raventree Hollow or in neighboring communities. These stories are all standalone tales, including my novel *Raventree Hollow*, so please don't feel that you need to read them in any kind of order to understand or enjoy them. They're all just stories in the same town where strange things happen. I have some reasons in my mind about why Raventree Hollow is the center of supernatural happenings (and seemingly plain old human evil), but it will be a while until all is revealed. For now, find a quiet place, a favorite beverage, and kick back and enjoy these tales.

A MACHETE & QUILL HORROR

DITCH

OF

THE

DAMNED

RYAN HOYT

Preface

This story came to me as a dream.

I've been planning a horror novel set in the 1800s American prairie since the summer of 2021, jotting down little tidbits in my notebooks that I'll eventually include. I went to bed in October 2022 thinking over those ideas, then slipped off into sleep. When I awoke the next morning, this story was almost completely formed. I remember dreams so rarely, sometimes just recalling the essence of a particularly vivid dream. This time, however, it was detailed. Alive. I had taken the week off of work to plug away at my novel *The Isle of Abandonment*, but instead I spent the morning recording my dream, almost exactly as I remembered it, filling in some missing details such as the characters' names.

I present to you my dark dream nearly as it came to me from that mysterious muse that serves us and feeds from our creative impulses. I hope you enjoy the story.

One

We were on our way west to start a new life when we stumbled upon a gateway to Hell. It was autumn of 1847. Pa said we should have arrived at our destination by then, lest we freeze to death somewhere in the Dakota Territories. He didn't know that there were other things to worry about. Things not of this world, or perhaps *more* of this world than the humans and animals that wandered it.

Pa and Uncle William pulled off the trail we'd been following for weeks. The wagon train sped on without us three days ago. To death with them. The other children were all troublemakers anyway, and I saw the way some of the husbands looked at Mama and me as if we were prime pieces of meat. Pa exchanged words with a man last week. Mr. Buchanan denied it, said the trail has gotten to Pa's mind and warped him. Mrs. Buchanan hurled all kinds of insults at me and Mama that I can't even repeat, and then they rode off with the other wagons, leaving us behind with our slow mules.

Now we're here with a broken wheel in Ravager Valley, or at least that's what Uncle calls it, but it isn't as if there are signs. That's the beauty of this place; it's all here for anyone to name. I know others must have seen it long before we rode through. We've seen them out behind the trees or up on the hills, watching us invade their lands. I wonder if they know we aren't here to hurt them, that we're just passing through. I wonder what names they've given to this valley.

These stops always took a few hours for repairs, so I did what I always do. I explored. I had the canteens with me, ready to fill them up if I could find a clean creek nearby. We did the washing on our last stop, so at least I didn't have to worry about assisting Mama with that for another few days. The ravine was slippery with all the loose pebbles, so I hunkered down on palms and feet and made my descent like a crab, four canteens dragging around me. A clear stream of water flowed just within the trees at the bottom. I dipped the first canteen in the frigid water. Snow had already fallen up on the peaks in the distance and this was the runoff.

I left my hand in the water. I liked when it went numb, like it was invincible to any harms of this world. Perhaps that is a strange way to feel considering what was to come. I was in a daze with the cool of the water, the pitter-patter of its flow through the mossy stones. I stared off into the trees, not quite seeing them, dreaming of whatever comfortable new home we were traveling toward.

A lapping sound pulled me out of it. As my vision

refocused, I peered straight across and locked eyes with it.

A dog. Only, I hadn't actually locked eyes with it. Its head was aimed toward mine, water dripped from its dangling tongue, but the beast looked through me. Was it also in a daze as I had been? No, it knew I was there but didn't meet my gaze. I splashed a hand across the surface of the stream, and the dog tilted its head a little to one side. I splashed again and it closed its mouth, whimpered, and returned to an open-mouth pant. That was when I understood. It had no eyes to see me with.

"Here, boy," I said, for I realized it was a male from the part between his legs. "It's okay. I'm a friend. Come on over to this side of the water!"

He whimpered again and lay down on his side of the muddy bank. I thought of crossing the stream to get to him, but evenings were too chilly for wet boots and stockings, and I didn't want to slice up my feet again on razor-sharp river rocks. I gathered the canteens and turned away from the dog and the water. I made my way back up the hill. Uncle William had propped up the wagon while Pa repaired the front left wheel. Mama was skinning the two rabbits Uncle had caught that morning on the trail.

"Where did you go, Eudora?" Mama asked. I winced at the blood that covered her hands as she worked at those poor little rabbits.

"Exploring. The hill was steep but not too bad. Down through the trees, I found—"

"You're filthy! I wish you had stayed to help. You'll be doing this for a husband of your own in no time."

"Damn it, Mina," Pa called from behind the wagon. Mina was short for Mama's actual name, Wilhelmina, and easier to yell in anger. "The girl is nine. Would you have her married off to an old creep like Buchanan already? Let her be a child, for the Lord's sake."

"I weren't much older than her when our fathers arranged our union, Charles. We may not be in Scotland anymore, but that doesn't mean things are different here."

"Only the willing need be chained to tradition," Pa fired back. "We have new opportunities here. We can do things how we want. We just need to open our eyes and our minds."

Mama shook her head, knowing Pa couldn't see her from the other side of the wagon. I knew other men would have struck their wives for such an act, but not Pa. He was a peaceable man. Ma set the furs aside and plopped the carcasses onto the cutting block. I turned away as she used the cleaver to spatchcock the rabbits. I tried to see through the trees down the hill to where the creek was and wondered if the dog was still there. We'd started our journey with a hound of our own. He had met his end when he came upon a bear along the trail. I missed our old Jack, and perhaps this could be our new Jack, even if he was blind.

Mama walked over to rustle through the cookware in a trunk from the back of the wagon. I rushed over to the raw meat on the cutting block and tore at it, but it was too tough. I picked up the cleaver and brought it down hard onto some part of the rabbit—I'd rather not know which—and winced as blood sprayed at me.

"What do you think you're doing, Eudora?"

I turned and stared at Mama for a second with two chunks of meat in my hand, apologized, and ran for the hill. I ignored her hollers as I made my way down again. I slipped twice but kept hold of the fleshy bits.

New Jack was still there, sprawled out on the muddy bank, licking his paws. He looked toward me as I approached my side of the stream, and it again struck me that he couldn't see. I tossed one of the pieces to him. It plopped with a sickeningly wet sound on the rocks between his front paws. New Jack sniffed it, licked, and then swallowed the meat whole.

"That's a good boy," I called. "I have more here. Do you want it? You must be hungry. Come on, Jacky-boy."

As if he'd already accepted the name, New Jack stood and sniffed the air. Not worried about soiling boots and stockings like I was, he crossed the stream. It wasn't too deep, only coming up a third of his legs in the center, and he made his way over easily. By the time he arrived at my side, I'd turned and headed toward the incline. I whistled every few seconds and glanced back to ensure he followed. The lure of the meat was enough. At the crest of the hill, I sat and let him catch up. He stopped just six feet away, hesitant to get any closer.

"It's okay, boy. I won't hurt you." I stretched my arm and held the second chunk of meat there for him. "Don't you want this? Come on over."

He whimpered and stepped cautiously toward me. He sniffed, bared his teeth, and snapped his face at the meat. I cried out as one of his teeth scraped a line of flesh from my thumb. I pulled back my hand once he'd taken the meat and I sucked at the little wound. Tears dripped down my cheeks, but I knew it wasn't New Jack's fault. He stood there staring at me, meat dangling from his jowls. He whimpered, dropped the meat, and stepped over to me. His tongue was warm on my cheek as he licked off the tears. I laughed and threw my arms around him. New Jack was a very good boy.

Two

"We're not keeping him, Eudora," Mama said. The repair complete, we were ready to get back on our way through the unending wilderness toward whatever future Pa promised lay ahead. I didn't care about the future, though. They'd had their own childhoods, and this was mine. My time. Why should it be spent wandering, searching for happiness when something that made me happy was sprawled out on the ground right next to me?

I fell over dramatically, rested my face on New Jack, and wept.

"We can barely feed the mouths we've got. I don't need another little beast to take care of, especially not after what happened to Jack. And this one, with his eyes sliced out like that, won't do us any good as a hunting hound. You may have given up your meals to him last night and this morning, but that's not going to last."

"Pa, please tell her we can keep New Jack!" I cried. I

knew Pa couldn't deny me of anything when I let the tears flow.

Pa slumped his head "I'm sorry, little love. Your mother is right. That mutt isn't what we need right now. He isn't fit to hunt. He'll only consume, not contribute, and we need all the help—and food—we can get for ourselves right now. With winter coming fast, we need to hurry on."

I brought my face close to New Jack's. I took in the place where his eyes had once been. The scars were from a blade, not from a bear's claw or a wolf's brutal teeth. Someone had mutilated him and left him to die alone in the wilderness. And here I was, another human to abandon him.

The ride was silent but for my weeping. New Jack had seemed to understand as we rode away. He faced our direction and listened as our wheels crunched over the trail. I imagine he just stood there as we faded off into the distance until he could no longer hear our wagon or our mules. I knew once he faded from view that I should no longer think of him as *New Jack*, but as *Jack That Never Was*.

Three

The wheel broke again the next morning, taking the entire axle assembly down with it. I won't repeat the words Pa and Uncle William used, but I will say they seemed terrified we'd never catch up to the rest of our party. Pa had wanted to make up for the previous day's lost time, so he and Uncle William had divided the night into shifts to keep the wagon moving. I always hated trying to sleep through all the rocking of our schooner, but I eventually let the darkness take me, only to wake up to the thud as the wheel detached.

As hard as I tried to forget about New Jack and move on, I was still upset with Mama. I wandered off with the canteens again, searching for a place to fill them. My mind and eyes were still cloudy from sleep, but I didn't want a lecture from Mama. I assumed the same stream from yesterday still flowed alongside the trail. I wanted desperately to find it and follow it back to where I'd found New Jack, though it pained me to think how badly it would hurt Pa if I were to run off.

The first grove of trees wasn't hiding the stream. Perhaps it was just a little farther on. I grimaced in pain as I took a step toward the next clearing. A pebble had lodged into my boot. I plopped onto a fallen tree trunk and pulled off the boot. That's when I noticed it wasn't a pebble at all. A jagged splinter of wood had punctured the pad of my boot, which was already falling apart even though Pa had paid a cobbler to fix it in the last town we'd passed through. I pulled the splinter out and looked over the pad of my foot. No puncture wound, no blood. I replaced the boot and retraced my steps back into the trees when something caught my eye.

A decaying board lay there among the leaves and grass. I must have stepped on it as I passed through a minute earlier. I leaned down and delicately picked it up, careful not to get slivers in my palms. It had bloated and rotted from the rains, but it seemed to have come from a wagon much like ours. It had been exposed to the elements for too long to have belonged to one of the wagons from the party that had abandoned us. I flipped it over to find a message scrawled in jagged red letters.

It was smeared, but I was quite certain of what it said:

Avert thine eyes
In these hills
For evil lurks
In the ditch that kills

I dropped the board and chuckled nervously. Why would anyone write such dark poetry on a board and leave it in the wild?

The morning sun shone through the canopy of trees and reflected off the canteens I'd left on the fallen tree. I collected them and moved on.

The stream was a little farther down. I made quick work of filling the canteens and continued on my way. Water flooded my punctured boot as I crossed the stream, but I didn't care. If New Jack could walk across the frigid stream with no hesitation, I could too. Once I made it to the other side, I whistled in the unlikely hope that the blind pup was near enough to hear. Perhaps his hearing had gotten stronger to make up for his loss of vision. Maybe he could smell me from miles away, what with the stench that emanated from me after days without a proper bath.

I walked for a quarter of an hour, doing my best to keep straight to the north, the sun still to my right. I went up and down a few hillocks covered in dried grasses, exposed to the sun without any trees for shade. The dirt gave way to rock. It felt like I was hiking boulders by that point.

That was when I stumbled upon the bowl of death. I don't know how else to describe it. Nearly a perfect circle of stony ground sloped down to a center. I'd have expected it to be an emptied pond, but I didn't know how any water would have sat undisturbed there, for there was a fissure in the stone almost directly in the center. I looked around the bowl, which was maybe twenty feet in diameter, and gasped. A rattler six feet to my right hadn't noticed me. I thought for a moment it was dead, but its head was up, its tongue popping in and out from between the fangs. I stepped to the left and jumped at the sound of a crunching beneath my feet. The skeletal remains of some kind of rodent.

I took in the rest of it: more bones scattered throughout; more dead animals not yet decayed; several rodents still breathing; two condors very much alive but completely ignoring the easy prey all around; two more snakes straight across from me; a variety of birds throughout. Every creature stared straight down to the center of the impression in the earth.

The ditch.

I stared back down at it, taking notice of the complete silence around us, save for the soft sound of a breeze. I must have been shielded from it where I stood, for I could only feel stillness in the air.

No, not a breeze. There was certainly no wind. It sounded more like...

Whispers.

They weren't speaking in any tongue I'd ever heard, yet in the depths of my heart I knew words were being repeated. Phrases, like near-silent prayers in a chapel of fifty folks with heads bowed, standing at their pews, all whispering some prayers to God above. Only there was nothing godly about this...

I took two more steps down to get a better look at the hole in the center. It wasn't a perfect circle, but rather like a careless tear from some giant beast, if such a mythical creature could even tear through stone like this. As I took one more step, the whispering grew louder. A shiver ran through me, and I dropped the canteens. The lid of one popped off as it hit the ground at just the right angle. The freshly collected contents poured out as the canteen slid down. The water flowed right down the giant bowl toward the fissure. I expected to hear the water splashing into a puddle, as surely rainwater had collected a couple feet down the pit, but it was only silence. The canteen continued its trajectory and disappeared into the maw. I heard it clanking against the edges. It went on for what felt like some time but was probably only a few seconds. Still, I never heard it hit the bottom; the sound simply faded out because it was too far away.

Impossible...

I braced myself then, expecting bats or birds to fly out following the intrusion of the foreign object, but nothing came. Just the impenetrable darkness of the hole, the constant whisper-like noise, and the stillness around me. I made to turn my head toward the rattler but found my neck wouldn't give. I tried to lift my right foot but couldn't. It didn't feel like anything had put weight or force on me to keep me in place, but more like my mind couldn't communicate with the rest of my body.

A tear dripped down my left cheek. I wanted to wipe it away because I didn't like the itchiness as it descended my face into the edge of my lips, but again I couldn't. That's when the rest of the tears came.

My eyes didn't leave the crack in the center. I just

stood there like those other animals, staring into the colorless void.

Hours passed. Long enough for my parents to get worried and come looking. Pa and Mama came together. I heard them calling but could not respond. Couldn't warn them. I wanted to tell them to turn away, to heed the warning of that sign. Mama found me and grabbed my hand, which moved as loosely in her grip as a garment in the wind, before she followed my gaze and froze next to me. Pa cried out at the strange sight. I heard him stepping toward us behind me before his voice cut off in an odd grunt, and he too froze in place.

Another couple hours passed. The sun had already worked its way overhead and was halfway to the west, that much closer to darkness. I didn't want to be out there when night fell. I didn't want to see if something crawled out of the depths in moonlight to collect its petrified prey. And I was hungry. So hungry. The growls from my stomach were almost a welcoming sound cutting through those incessant whispers.

Uncle William must have gone too far in a different direction, for he came over the crest of the bowl from the far side.

"There you are," he said. "Wagon is fixed now. It looks like another night of traveling under the stars. What the bloody hell are you all..."

He trailed off as he noticed we weren't moving. He witnessed the animals and the remains around us as well. He took another step over the rim of the bowl, but he caught loose gravel and slipped.

Uncle William came into my field of vision only

briefly as he slid on his side with a smattering of rocks and disappeared into the chasm. His screams seemed to last longer than the clanking of the canteen on its way down. I heard his body slamming against the walls as his cries grew quieter and more distant before they faded out entirely.

Goodbye, dear uncle. I'm sorry.

Four

Night fell.

The pain in my feet was unbearable, but there was nothing I could do. Mosquitos had their way with my flesh, yet I could not swat them away. Wolves howled nearby, though they seemed to avoid this spot. Perhaps I would have welcomed them if they wanted to feast on me. I knew deep in my gut that I would never leave the place alive, so why not make quick work of it and be done?

Nearer the howls got, but still not near enough. I wanted to scream, "Take me!" Would they have listened? Would they have braved the cursed place? Were they hungry enough to be irrational?

Another wolf howled.

No, not a wolf. And not as distant.

It was a bark. It was him. It *had* to be him.

Oh how I wanted to scream, to scare him away. If I died there, at least I would have died knowing he was spared, running free in the wilderness. If he came to me, he'd be in the same predicament.

His barks grew closer. Footsteps approached. Loose gravel slid down the curved stone floor around me.

New Jack whimpered behind me. His moist breath saturated my calves. I wanted to reach back and pet him, tell him he was a good boy, yet I also wanted to scare him away before he fell into this trap, but I could do none of these things.

He came around me and into view for the first time. His head lifted toward my face as if he could see me, but he had no eyes for that. New Jack crouched, then pounced straight at me. His weight easily knocked me off my weakened legs, and I tumbled backward. Without the ability to use my hands, I couldn't catch myself. The back of my head hit the ground hard and my consciousness left me.

Five

I awoke to New Jack's tongue lapping up the sweat and grease and tears on my face. I turned my head without realizing I was doing it. I moved my hands, used them to rub the wound on the back of my head where I'd slammed into the rocky surface of the bowl...

The bowl!

I was out of it. I saw that my dress was torn to shreds. Teeth marks had scraped into the skin, not quite to the bone, but deep enough to cause bleeding.

New Jack had dragged me out of the bowl.

Impossible? Yes, but there I was. Alive. A few feet outside of the rim. I looked around, careful to avoid staring directly into the dip in the earth. Nobody else was around. It had to have been New Jack. I thew my arms around him. He continued his kisses until I pulled back and looked at the spot his eyes had once been.

"Someone did this to you for a reason, huh boy?"

He whimpered back at me. I nodded in understanding. From my perch, I could see each of my parents from the shoulders up, still standing where they'd frozen.

I knew what I had to do. I tore at the hem of my dress, which had already long since tattered in our weeks on the trail. After a couple of failed attempts, I tore off a strip to fit over my eyes and around my head. I pulled it tight, then carefully crab-walked into the bowl and down, pausing momentarily to feel for Mama. When I reached her, I stood and wrapped an arm around her and gave a tender push. To my surprise, her feet moved. I guided her out and helped her to the ground, where she curled into a fetal position in half-consciousness. I did the same for my father, careful not to slip or accidentally run into him. To lose Pa the way we had certainly lost Uncle William would be as bad as having fallen into the pit ourselves. I likely would have thrown myself in at that point.

Fortunately, it didn't come to that.

We lay there until the morning light returned, huddled together: Mama, Pa, me, and and our pup, New Jack.

A MACHETE & QUILL HORROR

RYAN HOYT

A RAVENTREE HOLLOW STORY

SENIOR CLASS

Preface

I'm not done with Raventree Hollow yet. Like some of my favorite authors have done, I want this fictional town to feel alive. Lived in. Full of stories. There are so many people with tales to tell, houses that have played host to unspeakable horrors within their walls, monsters that lurk under the bed (or nestle within the innkeeper's head).

The evil in "Senior Class" is not the same entity as that which infects the townsfolk in the novel *Raventree Hollow*—or is it? What we have here seems much more human. Much more believable, perhaps. It's just one of many short stories, novellas, and novels I want to set in this afflicted small town, and I hope you'll continue to join me as I explore all of its shadowy corners.

Now, dust off your finest black loafers, follow the somber procession, and join us as we mourn another dearly departed citizen of Raventree Hollow...

One

Walter's funeral was a bore.

Pearl had lost count of how many she'd attended in her ninety-three years. Anyone that had made it that far had already buried their parents, spouses, even some children. Peers were dwindling. Everyone looked at survivors of that vintage and knew they'd be next in the ground. The plots of dirt in the cemetery were likely reserved already. The great-grandchildren were sending letters and flowers just often enough to be remembered in the will, but not so much as to appear obvious.

Pearl looked around the chapel and confirmed her suspicion that she was far from the only dry eye in the room. Just behind her, a man in his thirties—a great-nephew, Pearl guessed—kept his child occupied by passing a notepad back and forth with a game of hangman while the wife buried her eyes into a compact and touched up her lipstick. For a moment, Pearl half expected to see some of her old classmates, but then she remembered Walter *was* the only other classmate still in town.

The pastor sleepwalked through his part, a twenty-minute sermon Pearl had heard at least two dozen times over the last decade. He didn't bother to change it up; why fix what wasn't broken? Pastor Michael was nothing compared to the long-departed Pastor Laurence, but then he was just another of the things she'd outlived and seen replaced by something inferior.

The worn Bibles that resided in the backs of the stiff pews opened right up to each verse referenced, what with all the funerals over the years as Pearl's generation dropped like flies. In her boredom, Pearl moved her lips to recite each verse along with the pastor, not even bothering to glance down at the razor thin pages. She wouldn't have been able to read the text had she tried; Raventree Community Church didn't have the funds to invest in large-print copies to replace the ancient volumes that had survived most of Pearl's lifetime.

The real entertainment always started when the pastor called for family and friends to speak. Oh sure, there were always the same few sob-filled speeches from the remaining immediate family members. It was when the second cousins or the aforementioned great-nephews stepped up and pretended they knew anything about the dear departed that the laughs had to be stifled under Pearl's breath. She couldn't blame them, though; they were just trying to earn whatever pittance came their way when the estate was divvied up.

"Great-Uncle Walter... He was... He was great

indeed." It was the young man that had been sitting behind Pearl moments earlier. When he'd risen to his feet, Pearl had heard the notepad slip off his lap and fall to the floor. She'd turned back to see the man's wife reaching for his hand, trying to stop him from humiliating them. He'd brushed her off and made his way up to the dais. His smug look as he took to the pulpit like some charismatic preacher had faded once he realized he had nothing to say.

"When I was a child, um, I remember him always being so kind to me. He was... He was great." The man reached up and scratched his head, sending a sprig of his pomade-stiffened hair out of alignment. He realized, then tried to push it back into place while he pondered whether he had anything else to say. "I love you, Uncle Walter. I'll miss you." He blew a kiss toward the open casket, then jogged down the steps of the dais. The bit of hair rose back up and flopped around with each step.

Pearl could no longer contain her giggles. When she felt the attention on her, she did her best to turn them into sobs.

"Sister Pearl," Pastor Michael said from the pulpit, "you knew Walter longer than anyone in the room. Would you like to share any memories?" Even from halfway across the sanctuary, Pearl could read the expression on the pastor's face. He knew she'd been faking it. He'd witnessed enough of Pearl's dramatics at these semi-regular events that he could decipher her better than anyone.

She would not let him get the best of her.

Besides, she needed to get close to the body. She had

planned on collecting her souvenirs at the reception until she'd learned from the pamphlets in the church foyer that they would hold the reception in the court-yard instead of Walter's home. It would be a little more daring, but Pearl was feeling quite confident. They had never caught her before; why would this time be different?

Pearl made her way down the aisle, playing up each step to show her age and frailness. At one point she pretended to stumble, which did its job to provoke Carl Weathers to jump out of his seat and escort her the rest of the way up to the pulpit. Once there, Pearl made a show out of taking in the crowd. She furrowed her brow, then widened her eyes, looking lost. She turned her head toward the casket and dropped her jaw, as if she had just remembered where she was. That's when the waterworks started.

"I... I'm sorry," she uttered between artificial sobs. "Oh, Walter, my dear old friend! How I'll miss you!" Sympathetic *ooh*s and *aah*s sounded out from the congregants as Pearl waddled to the casket and wept over the body.

He never trimmed those nose hairs after all these years, she thought to herself as she eyed Walter's corpse. She passed over the gold chain that hung from a pocket of the suit and glimpsed the outline of the pocket-watch that attached to one end. *That chain might make too much noise if I try to unclasp it.* She moved her eyes farther down. Rings adorned three fingers on Walter's right hand.

His state championship rings, she realized. Walter had

been on the varsity football team for three years in high school, where he had contributed to their decades-long streak. She'd loathed football back then, almost as much as she'd loathed Walter himself, but nobody in the room knew that. Hell, the only person still alive that would have known that was Rosemary Richardson, and she hadn't been back to Raventree Hollow in decades.

Pearl threw herself down at the body and forced herself to tremble along with her loud sobs. She pressed her eyes together, hoping to draw out more phony tears, while her hands reached for Walter's bone-dry fingers. The rings on his pointer and ring fingers slipped right off, but the one on the gnarled middle finger wouldn't budge. She leaned in more, slipped the two she'd collected into her bosom, and let out another wail.

Footsteps approached her as she worked the remaining ring side to side, loosening the skin, straightening the finger. She heard a slight snap, felt a pop, as something gave way under the skin. A hand rubbed against her back with sympathy just as she made progress. The person's other hand took hold of her left shoulder and pulled her up off the casket. There was no time to slip the prize in among the other two. Instead, she worked it up onto her own finger. She turned, expecting to see Carl Weathers or Pastor Michael there to escort her back to her seat.

She gasped.

"Rosemary?"

"Hello, old friend." The other woman winked at Pearl, then crinkled her eyes in mock concern. "Let's get you on your way, dear."

Pearl kept her finger curled to ensure the loose ring stayed in place as she allowed her last remaining contemporary to guide her back down the aisle.

She found it harder than ever to keep up her mourning act now that she realized with pleasure that Walter would not be the only corpse from their graduating class to see six feet of dirt that week.

Two

The doorbell chimed at precisely eleven the following morning.

It was late in the day for Pearl, and she wasn't embarrassed to admit it. Ever since her mid-seventies, Pearl had found herself waking around three in the morning, still hours left until sunrise. She'd tried for months to continue lying in bed until dawn, forcing her eyes to stay shut, but could never escape back into slumber. She had taken to reading until she'd exhausted her modest library. Six months in, she had come to peace with her body's unwanted new schedule and was a quarter through her day before the sun had bothered to reveal itself. She'd found that the lines at the market were brisk at opening hour and that streets were wide open during her early neighborhood strolls. She had gained a new appreciation for her garden, already tended to by the time the flowers were ready to open for the day.

There were exceptions to her schedule, of course.

The occasional social visits. Dinner invitations. Distant relatives ringing on the telephone at what would be otherwise reasonable hours of the evening. The funerals, like Walter's the previous day.

By eleven in the morning, lunch was already behind her. It was time for afternoon tea on her schedule, and she would soon start preparing supper any other day. But today, there was company, and the company was punctual.

"Haven't changed, I see," Pearl said in greeting. "Rosemary Richardson, always on time."

Rosemary reached in and kissed both cheeks. "My dear Pearl, still as prickly as ever."

Pearl pulled back and rubbed her own cheek. She was uncertain if Rosemary was referring to her personality or the regretful little hairs that sprouted off her cheeks. That was something else that had started in her seventies, and Pearl had always regretted using a razor to slice the whiskers off. Once she'd begun doing that, she'd had to continue it weekly to save herself from becoming the bearded lady in some freak-show circus.

"I'm glad you're here," Pearl said as she swallowed down her scorn. She stepped aside for her visitor to enter. "When Matthew Anderson passed, I was certain you'd make it back to town for the funeral. The two of you were attached by the tongue in high school. And when Peggy Louise took ill and croaked, I thought for sure you would be there. Your co-captain of the cheer team and all."

Rosemary took a seat on one of the accent chairs next to the fireplace in the living room. Pearl plopped down across from her. "Pearl, high school was seventy years ago."

"Seventy-five," Pearl corrected. "You would have missed the reunion this year if there'd been enough of us left to plan it. Now you're here, so I guess this is it!"

"Yes, three quarters of a century. But after my family moved away from Raventree Hollow while I was in college, my life just wasn't here anymore. My high school sweetheart and my childhood best friend were just that: things of my youth. I hadn't thought of them in decades. We lived through countless wars. I had six children and buried four of them. They gave me seventeen grandchildren, and I've even outlived three so far. They shipped two more off to combat this year, so I'm not expecting to see them again."

"And yet you're here after Walter's passing. Why?" Pearl watched as Rosemary looked away. She seemed to stare at her warped reflection in the unpowered television screen across the room.

"It was you, Pearl. Your letters. You always let me know when one of our old compatriots passed. I always ignored the letters, used them as kindling in my furnace. But when I received the letter about Walter, I climbed up to the attic—not a great idea with these old hips, I'll tell you that—and dug out our senior class yearbook. I went through each picture one by one with a red felt pen. Drew an X over everyone that kicked the bucket over the years. With Walter crossed out, I realized something..." Rosemary trailed off.

"That there was only you and me left," Pearl finished

for her. Rosemary snapped out of her daze and turned back to Pearl.

"We were never friends back then," Rosemary continued. "It was always strange that you even wrote to me all these years. I don't know why you did it. Peggy Louise never bothered, nor Maryanne Kennedy, Patty Winchel, Susie Alcott. None of the girls I considered my closest pals as a child. Your letters were all I had to keep track of the news back home. You knew everything about everyone, it seemed. Raventree Hollow has always been big on gossip. It's much different from San Francisco. I don't know a single fact about my nearest neighbors other than which ones take an extra day to bring in their trash cans. But here, you seemed to document everything about everyone. So, with everyone else gone, I figured perhaps it was time to return and give you one last contemporary to write about."

Pearl gulped, then choked on her own saliva. Her dentures threatened to eject from her mouth before she regained composure. She stared hard into Rosemary's eyes. There was something knowing in them.

Could she know about…?

No. Nonsense.

The sound of the kettle in the kitchen broke the silence between the women.

"Well, I'm so glad you made that decision," Pearl said. She pushed herself up to her feet, knees cracking as her legs straightened. "What do you say we have some tea, my dear?"

Pearl made her way toward the kitchen without waiting for Rosemary to follow. As she pushed the swinging door inward to enter the kitchen, her companion's voice stopped her in her tracks. "What, no tour of your house?"

Pearl didn't look back. "You mean you haven't been here before? I doubt much has changed since our youth. My parents left the place to me, and I sure wasn't handy enough to do any big repairs or remodels. Without a husband or children of my own, I never had reason to."

"We were never friends, Pearl, so I didn't visit back then." Rosemary stood up and closed in on Pearl. She was agile for a woman of ninety-three. She pointed over Pearl's shoulder toward the bay window of the breakfast nook that overlooked the backyard. "What is that building out there?"

Pearl followed her gaze across the overgrown shrubbery, then glanced away. "Just the old barn. I'll show you later if you'd like." Pearl hustled toward the kettle, which was now at an intense boil, water spurting out of every crevice around the lid and spout.

"Would you like a hand?" Rosemary asked.

"Oh no, just go on through to the dining room and I'll bring out the tray."

Pearl opened a tin and gripped the measuring spoon, the dust of tea leaves pressing into the wrinkled pads of her fingers. She measured out a tablespoon into each infuser on the counter, latched the infusers, and set one in each teacup. She'd had to wash these cups, her only intact pair from a set of six that her mother had always prized. The rest had chipped or stained over the years, which hadn't ever bothered Pearl. She seldom entertained company. Pearl set the teacups onto the tray containing a little sugar dish, two teaspoons, and two saucers. She poured the scalding water into each cup, lifted the tray, then hesitated.

Pearl reached for a small bottle with a dropper, glanced behind her, then back at the bottle. She unloaded the contents of the dropper into one cup, then made her way into the dining room with the tray.

"This is lovely," Rosemary said, running her hand along the floral pattern on the tablecloth.

"Yes, I embroidered it myself. The tablecloth was Mother's, but the edges stained from use. I guess you could say I like to repurpose old things."

"You sure like to hold on to the past," Rosemary said. Pearl nearly dropped the tray. Rosemary jumped up to lend a hand. "Let me take that from you."

Pearl watched as her old classmate relieved her of the tray and set it down with a patronizing wink. She pulled out a chair and sat as Rosemary circled around to the other side of the table and took a seat directly opposite. Pearl glanced down at the teacups, then reached for the one she had intended for herself.

"Say, do you have any cookies?" Rosemary asked. "I only have a few of my real teeth left, but each one is a sweet tooth. Not much has changed in all these years."

Pearl rose and made for the kitchen. "I think I have some old biscuits that might still be good. Be right back."

Three

Ｔhe door swung shut.

Rosemary counted to three under her breath, then leaned across the table. She picked up the teacup from the saucer where Pearl had been sitting. She swapped it with her own, wincing at the clink of the cup on its saucer. Her bottom just met the chair when the door swung open again and Pearl passed through with a round tin of butter cookies.

"Ah, the old Christmas specials," Rosemary quipped. "Every year I exchange those cookie tins with my physician. I swear we just swap the exact two tins each time. And yet if I were to break the seal and reach for a cookie, it would be just as crisp as the day they made them."

Pearl laughed at that. Rosemary was relieved that the woman seemed to relax. She'd been on edge ever since Rosemary had pointed out the barn. Rosemary had realized that it was a stupid thing to do. She had tipped her own hand by calling attention to it.

Across the table, Pearl pried off the lid, then tipped the tin toward Rosemary. "Still look crisp and buttery to me," she said with a smile.

Rosemary reached across the table and grabbed a cookie shaped like a small pretzel. She watched as Pearl grabbed one with tiny chocolate chips and dunked it into the steaming tea. Rosemary took a nibble of her own cookie, set it on the saucer, and picked up the tea.

"To old times," she said.

Pearl met her gaze and lifted her own cup. "And to the future."

Rosemary took a sip, keeping her eyes open and fixed on her companion. Pearl did the same. Their shared gaze seemed to trouble Pearl.

Rosemary pulled her lips from the rim of the cup and smiled at Pearl. "Delicious tea."

Pearl continued sipping, steam fogging her spectacles. When she set the cup down, her brow furrowed in concern.

"Pearl, what's the matter?"

"Did you switch the teacups?"

"What if I did?" Rosemary asked. "What if I knew what you were going to do?"

Pearl pushed her chair away from the table. "You were always a stupid girl, Rosemary. Thought you were smarter than everyone else, but you never were."

A fog rolled over Rosemary's vision. She tried to stand, but her legs didn't seem to listen. That's when it hit her. "No…"

"Oh, yes," Pearl said. A devious grin crossed her face. "Yes indeed."

Four

Walter had suspected it first. He'd reached out to Rosemary out of the blue twelve years ago. She had been shocked to have received his call, but she had also flushed with excitement when he gave his name. His voice had gone deep and gruff over the years. It was quite sexy. His cadence hadn't slowed at all. He was still the same fast-talking boy from high school that could get himself out of any kind of trouble—or into any girl's skirts.

"You'll never believe this," he said. And she didn't believe it. She nodded along, tossed out the necessary *you can't be serious* or *no way* as he went on and on about all the deaths of their classmates. He claimed the situations around so many of their old peers' passings were unusual. Planned, even. Plotted and executed by a serial psychopath.

He called her several times each year after that, updating her on the latest deaths just as she read the letters from Pearl about the same happenings. Every time, he provided more outlandish tidbits about the occurrences. Mickey's new deck collapsing from under him. The wheels of Sal's coupe coming clean off on the highway despite his years as a mechanic. Melissa's drowning at the senior center pool during a water aerobics class where Pearl had been the only other person attending, and the instructor had been conveniently sent to the locker room to find Pearl's inhalers.

It wasn't until two weeks before his death when Rosemary started to believe him.

"I'm the only one left, Rose! Just me and her. I saw her outside my house this morning. Half past four. Still dark out. She was peeking in my windows."

"And what were you doing up at that hour, you old geezer?"

"It's my bladder, Rose. Keeps waking me up every hour. I heard someone walking over the leaves in the side yard just as I was about to flush. I tiptoed out to the kitchen and crouched behind the counter. The beam of her flashlight barely swept over my head through the window. The light reflected off the glass right back onto her face. Saw her clear as day."

"And you think she's coming for you?"

"I do. This is goodbye, Rosemary. I've always loved you. Matthew Anderson didn't deserve you back then. It should have been me."

"Goodbye, Walter," she said and hung up.

She regretted the way she ended the call the moment the letter arrived from Pearl about a week later.

There   was   a   flight   from   San   Francisco

International Airport leaving only hours later. The cost of a ticket was as much as her Social Security check, but she had no other choice. She made it just in time, flew in, took the train the rest of the way into Raventree Hollow, and avoided anyone who might have recognized her.

The morning of Walter's funeral, she waited in her rental car at the mouth of Pearl's cul-de-sac. A taxi passed her, picked up Pearl, and passed again on its way to the church.

Rosemary tugged at the string through the fence and was relieved to find the gate was unlocked. She made her way to the back door but wasn't as fortunate. It didn't budge. She checked under the floor mat and nearby flowerpots, but there didn't appear to be a spare key. Then something had caught her eye.

Across the yard was a structure. It was quite an odd shape for a barn or shed, a pure triangle. It looked ancient, even older than the house itself.

That was when the dread washed over her.

She crossed the yard. Opened the door. Saw all that was on display.

She wanted to vomit but swallowed it down and ran back to her car. She arrived at the church just in time to witness Pearl's little show, crying over the casket of the man she had murdered.

After the funeral, Pearl invited her over for tea the following morning. That would be it. The moment of truth, when Rosemary would have to face her fate or carve out her own future.

The next morning came. The awkward small talk.

Pointing out the triangular structure through the window.

The tea.

She was ready for it. Really, what else could the frail old woman have been planning? It had to look natural. *Of course* it was going to be poison in the tea.

And so she sent Pearl out of the room. She switched the cups.

She drunk the tea.

<h1 style="text-align:center">Five</h1>

"Now dear, mind the bumps."

Rosemary's consciousness returned like a series of sparks out of the darkness before it ignited in full. She was moving, but not of her own volition.

She looked down.

A wheelchair.

Pearl was pushing her across the moss-covered steppingstones through the backyard.

Toward the barn.

"Nnn..." Rosemary tried to speak, but her mouth felt as if it were filled with cotton. "No..."

She came to a halt in front of the doors. Pearl came up from behind the wheelchair and opened them. Then she went back to the handles, popped the wheelchair up on the two rear wheels, and pushed it over the threshold.

The place reeked like mothballs. When Rosemary had entered it the first time the previous morning, she'd been astonished to find the place free of dust. It was like a museum, kept so pristine by those that dedicated their lives to preserving its artifacts.

The bumper of Sal Halstrom's car with its sticker advertising his auto mechanics business. Peggy Louise's pompoms, looking as perfectly frilly as they had at the start of the homecoming game in senior year. Two dozen other mementos. Some she didn't recognize on sight alone, but each had a placard next to it, emblazoned with the name and yearbook photo of each original owner.

Nearest her, on what appeared to be a newly acquired table with a bright lamp shining straight down on them, were three rings. Walter's rings. Polished, sparkling as they did each of those years when the boys had taken their state championships.

She looked to her right. There was a display case.

Empty except for the placard.

The name read *Pearl Songstrum* and was accompanied by an ancient picture of the killer, glasses shaped like cat's eyes affixed to her face by strings attached behind both ears, hair permed, makeup applied with inexperienced hands.

"That's where I intended for you to place my memento. Though, to be honest, I couldn't quite decide on what it should be. I've spent my entire life treasuring little trinkets from every other person in our graduating class. I never had a unique calling card. Nothing everyone knew me by. I figured you'd be able to find something in the house when you finished out the collection."

"Me? Why me?" Rosemary asked. She shifted in her wheelchair, trying to face Pearl. Her captor turned the chair for her.

"Well, I worked so hard on this for seventy years. Kept it nice. Kept it secret. Ensured I had new pieces to add every so often, but rarely enough to show a pattern. But I nearly failed with Sam Harris, about a month before Walter. I should have been better, but I've been getting these migraines. I saw a doctor about them a couple of weeks ago, and he diagnosed me with a brain tumor. Too far along to operate. A month left to live, maybe two at most."

Rosemary had no desire to express condolences. Pearl didn't deserve the respect.

"So, I figured if I couldn't enjoy this, I'd finish off Walter and then let you in on the secret. If you showed up, that is. To get you here, I first had to let Walter see me. He's been on to me for some time, I know it. Once he contacted you, I threw in all my chips. Got rid of him."

"You maniac," Rosemary spat.

"Yes, but it worked. Here you are."

"But you killed me instead."

"You did that to yourself. I meant for you to watch me drink that poison. I had my confession planned. I had always been an outcast in school, never belonging. I was finally going to fit in with the rest of the class at the end. Instead, I need to make up a new placard with your name and picture."

Sweat streamed down Rosemary's face as the poison worked through her bloodstream. "And what's my ultimate memento for your sick little display? You have nothing of mine in this twisted town."

Pearl giggled, sounding as Rosemary remembered the awkward little girl that she and her friends had always laughed at in childhood.

"The morning I let Walter catch me, I'd already been into his storage shed. He never got over the heartbreak of losing you, it seems."

"We never dated," Rosemary managed in a harsh screech. "Matthew was my boyfriend all during high school."

"Oh, but there were secret letters, weren't there? I know so. Walter kept every single one. Just in the slightest chance things went wrong with my plan, I knew I would at least have a backup."

"No!" Rosemary tried to shout, but it came out as a whisper. Her lungs gave out.

She heard Pearl one last time before the darkness overtook her.

"My collection is complete."

A MACHETE & QUILL HORROR
BUTTER SCOTCH
A RAVENTREE HOLLOW STORY
RYAN HOYT

Preface

This is the second short story that came to me almost fully formed as a dream. It's rare I wake up and remember a dream so clearly, so I knew I had to write down every detail immediately that morning, even if I was late for work.

I think this story stemmed out of my anxieties about moving away from my hometown for the first time in my life. It came to me within a week after my wife and I had an offer on a house accepted and the reality hit me that we were leaving everyone I've ever known.

I enjoyed adding some personal easter eggs for my family as well. The mannerisms of the daughters are based very much on my daughters. The candy dishes are straight out of the sepia-toned memories of my grandma's and great-grandma's homes. I can feel the textures of those dishes and taste the variety of those little hard candies right now as I reminisce about them.

The decision to set the story in the town of Raventree Hollow came as I wrote it. I wanted to use that town as a stage for more scary and twisted tales, and this felt like the perfect opportunity. I wrote "Senior Class" a few months after this one, and that was also set in Raventree Hollow, but neither story is a sequel to the other, nor to the novel *Raventree Hollow*. That said, there are some fun little easter eggs for you if you've read that novel. Either way, I hope you have a great time reading "Butterscotch." Enjoy.

Chapter One

A cloud of dust wafted into Danny Kauer's face as he opened the front door for the first time, cementing his first impressions of the new house. The sticky, unseen wall of webbing that clung to him three steps into the foyer just hammered it all home.

Home.

What a concept it was. What a home it was, this dilapidated Victorian house in a dilapidated town. Chrissy had called it an antique, just in need of a slight polishing around the edges. It was also the best they could do anywhere within the commuter corridor of the big city. An hour by over-packed train or about the same in bumper-to-bumper traffic up the two-lane highway, pick your poison. The rent on their one-bedroom apartment in the city had crept up beyond the cost of a reasonable suburban mortgage, and their two girls had long outgrown the living room-turned-bedroom. This house had a lot going for it on paper.

Chrissy had made a half-dozen trips out to see it and other homes, but after offers fell through on two newer homes in Raventree Hollow, this was lucky number three.

Danny dropped his duffel bag on the hardwood floor, launching another gray dust cloud.

"What a dump!" Danny turned and nodded in agreement with his oldest daughter. They locked eyes and laughed together until Danny abruptly cut Olivia off with a pointer finger in front of his lips.

"We're home, guys," Chrissy said as she came up the porch and scooted past Olivia through the door. Liz followed, her face buried in a graphic novel. If Danny had to guess, he'd say Liz's eyes hadn't even caught sight of the house yet. He reached over and yanked the book from her hands as she trudged past him.

"Hey!" Liz called out. "I was..." Her face scrunched in disgust as she trailed off. "Wait, where are we?"

"This is our new place, baby," Chrissy said. The pride was evident on her face. The condition of the place hadn't fazed her as it had the rest of the family—and any other prospective homebuyers that had likely hit the gas pedal as soon as their eyes had shifted from the *For Sale* sign to the sagging beast looming over it.

"Come on, let's pick out our room!" Olivia said as she took her little sister's hand. The two ran up the stairs despite the groaning of each board they stomped over in their ascent. Their apprehension seemed to lift as excited *oohs* and *aahs* sounded out when they took in the size of the bedrooms.

"I still can't believe they want to share a room again

when we finally have more than enough for everyone," Danny said.

Chrissy took Danny's hand and spun him around for a kiss. She was so ecstatic that Danny had no other choice but to smile at her as their lips parted. "What do you think of the place?" she asked.

"I think I'm looking forward to our first night together here. Maybe a wall that's not shared with the kids' room," Danny said. Chrissy punched his arm playfully and closed the front door before pulling him through the living room, past the stairs, and through a swinging door.

"We finally have a table that fits us and the kids and any guests." She gestured at the long dining table, storm-cloud gray with the requisite layer of dust. A porcelain tea set adorned the center of the tabletop, with the beam of sunshine cutting through the window, illuminating the thin webs strung between each little cup.

"Did the staging company leave this here?" Danny asked.

"The previous owner did. We'll use our own beds and our old couch and all that, but at least we won't have to buy anything to fill the rest of the space."

"We'll absolutely need a new vacuum. Ours will break down after cleaning just one of these rooms. How long has it been empty?"

Chrissy answered, but Danny's attention was pulled away. A hutch hulked over the other side of the table, the kind both sets of his grandparents used to store the fine china they never let him or his brothers eat from at family gatherings. This one looked quite old, but not fancy. It had been repainted at least once over the years with the wrong kind of paint, probably whatever was left over in a can in the back of a storage shed. The sheen was too high for furniture, and drops caked up on the corners and ledges. Chrissy continued her story about the previous owner, but Danny made his way around the table, pushing in the chairs as he passed them. His eyes were fixed on the cabinets in the lower half of the hutch.

Danny crouched down and pulled open the three cabinet doors. Each one stuck at first, gummed up with the sloppy paint job, but a little force did the trick. He brushed away a trio of dried-up earwigs with one hand and scooted back to take in the contents of the cabinets.

"Beautiful crystal dishes," Chrissy said, cutting off her own story. She knelt down next to Danny and rummaged through the items.

"Great-Grandma Dorris had a few just like this," Danny said, pulling out a small dish.

"Did she smoke? Everyone smoked in those days, I guess."

"It's not an ashtray," Danny said. He took a deep breath and blew out more long-deceased insects from the bowl. It was translucent, but had a yellowed amber tint with a raised pattern of leaves and flowers. "It's a candy dish. She always had little hard candies in these, sitting out on the coffee table, the dining table, even on top of the old boxy television set. They were everywhere."

"The candies with the little strawberry wrappers?"

A boyish smile spread over Danny's face. "Exactly! They always looked more exciting than they tasted. And there were the coffee ones, and—"

"—the butterscotch," Chrissy finished for him.

"The absolute worst!" they said in unison. Chrissy's giddiness about the house was contagious, and Danny finally gave in to the excitement. He pulled her in for a kiss and they toppled onto the filthy ground. Their lips met for only a second before thick chimes somewhere in the walls sounded out.

"What the hell is that?" Danny asked.

"A real doorbell! None of that electronic chime crap. Told you this place is an antique."

"A real gem…"

"Let's see who our first visitor is," Chrissy said. She jumped to her feet and grabbed Danny's right hand, nearly dragging him as he scrambled to get off the chair-scraped hardwood floor. He kept the dish in his left hand.

"Probably just the neighborhood welcome party. Maybe armed with a fresh-baked pie."

"Cookies," Chrissy called back. "Seriously, who bakes pies anymore? Too much—aah!"

Her scream as she yanked open the door caused Danny to stumble into an orphaned coffee table in the living room. Pain shot up his leg as his shin met the sharp corner. He dropped the dish onto the low table and looked across the room to the newly opened door.

A man stood there in what must have once been full clown makeup, but sweat had mangled the exaggerated features. A trail of red that had outlined his face and hairline now slopped down his forehead and neck. He was flanked by two young boys in grotesque rubber masks with fake bloody gashes, rotted teeth, and bruised circles around yellowing eyes, with small hidden slits for their sight and oxygen.

"Trick or treat!" the kids shouted with excitement unbefitting of their dour costumes. Their father took a quick step back when he realized he had terrified Chrissy. He broke into a hearty laugh.

"Woah, neighbor!" the man said. "Didn't mean to terrify you, but I can imagine how ghastly I must look right now. This humidity is unheard of so late in the fall. I'm sweating right through my costume." The boys pulled off their masks, their hair and cheeks drenched with perspiration. The smell wafted into the room and hit Danny.

"We forgot all about Halloween," Chrissy said, looking back at her husband.

"Sure did," Danny said. He trotted across the room toward the door. "We just arrived a few minutes ago. Lost track of the calendar with all the packing and moving preparation these last couple of weeks."

The boys groaned with disappointment as their father's smile faded. "Well, I suppose that's understandable," the clown said. "Though you should be aware that small towns like Raventree Hollow take holidays quite seriously, and Halloween just as much as any other. Gonna get quite a few upset families like mine tonight."

"We're so sorry," Chrissy offered. Danny sensed her positivity level sinking and put his arm around her shoulder. "Like my husband said, it's been a lot to move our family to a new town. We have two girls, probably around the same ages as your boys, eleven and nine. They're so excited to have their own room and—"

"Very upset families," the man continued, as if he couldn't hear Chrissy talking. "A few decorations go a long way, but what the kids really want is candy. Boy, I'd hate to be a dentist on this fine night, but it only comes around once per year." His eyes drifted between Danny and Chrissy into the mess beyond.

Danny turned to take in the view of the living room. "Yeah, we just got here, so we haven't had a chance to clean up yet. Kind of thought maybe the realtor would have at least dusted before the sale went through."

The clown pushed through his sons and took a step up into the doorway. "Oh!" Chrissy uttered in surprise. She stepped back. Danny turned toward the man.

"We're not quite ready for visitors just yet, mister...?"

"Quentin. Albie Quentin." His speech slowed, almost to a drunken slur.

"Maybe next week, then, Albie."

"Next... Week..." Albie took another step through the foyer toward the living room and froze, his jaw agape, eyes fixed on the coffee table. Danny locked eyes with Chrissy and furrowed his brows. Chrissy shrugged. He turned his attention back to their visitor and placed his hand on the man's sweat-soaked shoulder. Albie jumped as if shaken out of a dream.

"Are you okay, Albie?"

"Fine, just fine. Say, is there any candy to go with

that dish? Perhaps that would suffice." He gestured to the kids who stood like sentries on the porch. "For the children. Halloween and all. Must have something that belongs in a dish like that."

"Sorry," Chrissy said. "Like we said, we don't have anything to give at the moment."

"Oh, maybe a granola bar?" Danny offered. He started toward the duffel bag he'd dropped when he first arrived. "Pretty sure I have a couple in my overnight pack here."

"No, that's alright," Albie said. A good-natured smile returned under the array of colors smeared across his face. "No treats needed after all." He walked out the door as quickly as he'd entered and waved for his children to follow him down the porch steps. He turned his head toward the couple. "And welcome to the neighborhood. You're going to love it in Raventree Hollow!"

Danny and Chrissy watched as the trio made their way down the concrete path, through the gate, and down the sidewalk to their next destination.

"What the hell is wrong with this place?" Danny asked, then "Ouch!" as Chrissy backhanded him in the same spot on his upper arm where she'd punched him a few minutes earlier. He followed her back inside after securing the bolt on the door and the lock on the knob. He paused for a moment and stared at the candy dish, then trailed behind his wife on a tour of the rest of their new house.

Chapter Two

S*critch.*

Danny opened his eyes. Moonlight shone in through the uncovered windows. Curtains were high on their shopping list for the next morning, along with candy and actual necessities. He took in the sight of his wife asleep next to him. The puddle of drool on her pillow was evidence that she hadn't moved in quite some time. He sat up and looked around. The movers had arrived that evening just after the awkward first meeting with the neighbors, and now boxes were strewn all around, waiting to be unpacked. Beds and blankets were the first priority; the rest of it could wait until the days to come.

Scriiiitch.

That sound again, only longer this time. Movement. Danny turned toward one window, following the motion. Black. Quick. Ears and a tail. A rat? No. A shadow of something larger. He pivoted his gaze toward the window and jumped at the sight of the yellow eyes that met his. Just as quickly, the creature was gone.

He stepped down, the grittiness of debris on the splintered hardwood floor making him wince. Rugs were also high on their shopping list until they could afford a carpet installer to come in and work their magic. Danny navigated around the maze of boxes until he reached the window. The two latches snapped open with some effort, and he pulled the lower half up. The cool breeze was relieving as it mingled with the sweltering upstairs heat.

Danny stuck his head outside. Something jabbed between his eyes, causing him to flinch. He slammed the back of his head into the window frame. He pulled himself back inside and rubbed his head, swearing softly.

Something stirred in the room behind him. He turned to see Chrissy rolling away from the moonlight seeping in through the window, but still very much asleep. The shadow moved along the wall beyond the bed. Danny spun around and screamed as the figure lunged at him.

The front claws slashed his cheeks open. He threw his head back, narrowly avoiding the snapping jaw. He grasped the dark gray fur in both hands and threw the thing at the floor.

Mmraarrr, it bellowed as it hit the ground and darted toward the closed door. It stood on its hind legs and scratched at the door with its front claws. *Scritch.*

"Honey, what's wrong?" Chrissy asked, darting up and throwing the sheets off.

"Just a cat. I need to see if I can get it out of here without losing an eye." Danny rubbed at his cheeks and winced at the blood illuminated by the moonlight. "I must look like that clown that came to the door earlier."

"Why are you letting cats into the house?"

"It was scratching at the window. I didn't know what it was at first, and then it just attacked me and invited itself in."

"They."

"What?" Danny turned around to see two more cats pacing between the boxes. One was jet black, the other stark white with blood-red eyes. "Just great..."

"Open the door and let them roam around until morning. The girls closed their door when they went to bed, so they'll be safe."

Danny obliged. As soon as he pulled the door open, all three felines darted into the darkness beyond. Danny made sure the door clicked shut again and returned to bed. He mentally added *new sheets* to his shopping list, as these would be covered in blood by morning.

Chapter Three

"Daddy, you're the best!"

Liz cannon-balled into the narrow gap in the bed between Danny and Chrissy. It wasn't every day that Danny woke up to compliments. Usually, his kids started the days off with complaints about being hungry for breakfast, or cries over whose turn it was to pick the video game.

"You love the house that much?" Danny mumbled through his pillow. He lifted his face and winced as his cheek peeled off the pillow, sprinkling bits of dried blood.

"No, it's all dirty and nasty, but I love the cats that much!" Liz bounced, sending shockwaves across the mattress. "Oh, and Olivia said we should all get Tetris shots before we die from rusty nails."

"Tetanus," Chrissy corrected as she wiped the sleep from her eyes.

"Tetris sounds more fun, though," Danny said. He

pulled away the sheets and got out of bed. Liz pounced off the mattress and wrapped herself around him, sending him stumbling toward the window and reminding him of the night visitors. "Now let's go find a broom to shoe those cats away with."

"But can't we keep them, Daddy?"

"Absolutely not," Chrissy called. She pulled the sheets over her head in an attempt to extend the night's sleep.

Liz pointed the way as Danny carried her down the stairs and into the dining room. Olivia sat at the head of the dusty table, a spoonful of peanut butter in front of her gaping mouth. She dropped it back into the container in front of her. "Couldn't find the cereal," she said.

"Upper shelf, left of the fridge," Danny said.

"Or the bowls."

"Lower cupboard, also left of the fridge." Danny set Liz down.

"Anyway, we never bought new milk." Olivia grabbed her spoon in apparent victory and took another bite of the peanut butter.

"Fair enough," Danny conceded. "Save some for me if it's crunchy. None of that creamy junk. Now, where are those little fleabags?" He followed Liz around the table.

"They've been doing this all morning," Liz said. Danny followed her gaze toward the three cats, each scratching away at the cabinet doors of the hutch. For as small as the felines were, their claw marks looked downright leonine. "We tried stopping them, but they hissed at us."

"Mom's going to be pissed," Olivia said.

"Don't say pissed," Danny said.

"Will she get soap in her mouth?" Liz asked hopefully. Olivia catapulted a chunk of peanut butter in retaliation.

"No, but she's right. Mom loved how antique this hutch was." Danny crouched down cautiously, aware he was placing himself in striking distance in case the cats wanted another chance to mess up his face. "Maybe they smell a rat in here or something." He reached for the center cabinet door and hooked a finger through the brass loop that hung down on one side, but hesitated.

"What's wrong?" Olivia asked from the table.

"It sounds stupid, but something about this hutch seemed to call out to me when I walked in to this room for the first time. Seems like it's doing the same to these cats."

"Yup, pretty stupid," Liz said. "I'm already eight and even I know furniture can't talk."

Danny chuckled at that as he tugged at the brass ring. As soon as the cabinet door was opened far enough, the cats leaped inside. An empty flower vase rolled out of the darkness within. Several other glass items clinked together as the three cats paced around the small space in their hunt, but no rats jumped out into the light.

Scritch

"What are you guys thinking?" Danny asked as he

pulled the other two cabinet doors open for a better look. The cats were scratching away at the back wall of the cabinet.

"I see something," Liz said. She reached into the cabinet, but Danny stopped her.

"Those creatures will slice your little fingers right off." He offered his own hand as a sacrifice instead. He closed his pointer finger and thumb around a tiny brass knob and pulled. The false wall came off as a one foot tall by two foot wide wooden board painted to match the rest of the hutch. A slim space no more than three inches deep was revealed between the false wall and the actual back of the cabinet.

A purple felt bag sat hidden within the gap.

The cats pounced at the bag, but Danny was quicker. He slammed his head on the top of the cabinet as he pulled back and jumped to his feet. He held the bag in front of his face and analyzed it. It had a gold drawstring. Some kind of lettering on the fuzzy purple sack had flaked off over the years, leaving a smattering of faux-gold dots that Danny was quite certain had spelled out the name of an alcohol brand he couldn't recall. It reeked like an old suit hanging from a thrift store rack and immediately brought to mind the baby-blue tuxedo he'd seen his father don in photos from the old man's high school prom.

"Is it treasure?" Liz asked.

"As if anything valuable would have been left in this old dump," Olivia said. One of the cats meowed, seemingly in agreement. It jumped up on to the table and stared up at the sack. The other two followed its lead.

Danny cupped the bag with his other hand and closed his fingers around the bottom. Plastic rustled from inside. He grunted in confusion. "Only one way to find out." He gripped the lip of the bag with both hands and tugged at it, causing the drawstring to retract. He turned it upside down and let the contents spill out onto the table. They landed with a soft thud.

Danny, his daughters, and the cats stared at the contents on the table, dumbfounded.

"Are those—"

The doorbell cut Olivia's words short.

"Hard candies," Danny answered, unfazed by the chiming from the front room. "Butterscotch of all flavors."

"So definitely not treasure?" Liz asked.

"Then why did someone go through the trouble of hiding them?" Olivia asked.

"And why did the cats want them?" Danny looked at the strays on the table. The candies were fully within reach of the cats. Danny had no interest in sacrificing the skin on his forearms to guard the candies, but the cats made no attempt to claim their prize. One of them turned and sniffed at the open peanut butter jar in front of Olivia at the other end while the other two stared up at Danny as if assessing his reaction.

"I think they just wanted us to find them," Liz said. She picked up one of the cats without fear, bringing it against her chest and nuzzling her face into its fur. "How sweet of them."

The bell chimed again. "I better get that," Danny said. He turned and pushed his way through the swinging door into the living room. One of the cats darted through as the door rebounded in the opposite direction and followed Danny to the foyer.

"Trick or treat!" two boys called out when Danny opened the door. The Quentin kids stood on the porch, adorned in black football jerseys with crimson letters that spelled out *Raventree Krakens*.

"Hello again, neighbor!" Albie said from behind his sons. No clown makeup this time, but he wore a black-and-white striped referee shirt with a whistle hanging from his neck. "Thought we'd try again since last night was such a bust."

Danny sighed. "I'm sorry, boys, but after the moving truck was unloaded, we went to bed. No time to hit the grocery store."

"That's just too bad," Albie said. "Children are so easily disappointed, as I'm sure you must know." His eyes dropped from Danny, who followed the man's gaze down to the cat. It hissed at Albie and then disappeared into the maze of boxes that filled the living room.

"Sorry, don't mind him. Testy little fellow."

"Didn't realize you had a cat," Albie said. His voice had slowed to a dazed cadence. His eyes met Danny's again, but there was something off about them all of a sudden. *Tired*, Danny thought. *Lifeless*.

As much as Danny had wanted to get rid of the cats just minutes earlier, he suddenly felt protective of them. He leaned into the doorframe and pulled the door against him to block any view into the house. "Yeah, we seem to have adopted three of them. Cute creatures. Gentle," he said, rubbing his cheek. "Mostly."

The two boys took a step forward, so suddenly that Danny stumbled backward. The door flew open at the motion and the boys walked past him. "Trick or treat," they called into the house. They stomped into the living room and stopped at the coffee table. Their heads turned every which way, as if they could find candy hidden somewhere in the room.

Olivia and Liz pushed through the swinging door from the dining room. "Hello," Liz said. She introduced herself to the boys, who acted as if she wasn't there.

"You're supposed to say hello back," Olivia lectured, but the boys continued their scan of the room.

"Rude," Liz said.

"You know, I'm quite sure old Barry Stetson had three cats when he lived here." Albie stepped through the front doorway uninvited, following his sons into the living room. "He had an unquenchable sweet tooth as well. He was just like a child with his love for candy. Had more than enough to share with all the kids in the neighborhood." Albie bent over and picked up the empty candy dish from the coffee table.

"Please be careful with that," Danny said. He wasn't sure why he felt possessive of the dish. It hadn't even belonged to him before yesterday.

"Mr. Stetson had a dozen of these. Set them out on every surface. Mounds of sweets piled in each one. He was quite hospitable for a time." Albie's expression turned dark. "Until he wasn't."

"Hey!" Liz yelled as the boys pushed past her, bumping shoulders on their way through the swinging door. Danny jogged across the room and followed the kids into the dining room.

"Wait, it's a mess in there. We weren't expecting company. We just—"

Danny cut himself off at the sight of the table. The peanut butter jar still sat there, the lid screwed on and Olivia's spoon resting on top. The rest of the table was covered in nothing but dust, though Danny spotted a section that looked as if it had been brushed off by a small pair of hands. He looked back at Liz, who winked.

"Just wanted to dust in here before we had company, that's all," Danny finished. The boys looked at him, unconvinced. One turned and looked around the at the top shelves of the hutch, then knelt and pulled the cabinets open. He pulled out dish after dish, all empty, and set them on the floor. Convinced there was nothing of interest to him, he stood back up. His face drooped as if he were about to cry.

And then the cats pounced.

The two still in the dining room dug their claws into the boys' legs below their shorts. Albie screamed from the living room as the third cat had its way with him.

"Daddy!" one of the boys called. He ran into the living room, followed closely by his brother. The cats pursued them up to the swinging door, which was held open by Olivia, and hissed at their prey. The boys' father stumbled toward the door and kicked his leg out to put distance between him and his furry attacker.

"Mr. Stetson showed much more hospitality than this!" Albie shouted as he ushered his boys outside and slammed the door behind them. The cats ceased their hissing as soon as the Quentin family had stomped off down the path and through the front gate.

"What in the hell was that all about?" Liz asked.

"Mr. Stetson." Everyone turned toward the stairs, where Chrissy had stopped halfway through her descent to witness the commotion. "Whoever he is, this is all about him. We have to find Mr. Stetson."

Chapter Four

Locating Barry Stetson's whereabouts wasn't so difficult. Danny had gone down to the grocery store for milk and other essentials—no candy, though—and asked the clerk about the man while he paid for the goods. The clerk had shot a frightened look at him from the mention of Stetson's name, then shook her head as if she hadn't a clue who he was.

"I know him," the man in line behind Danny had said. Danny turned to face the speaker, a frail old gentleman with cola-bottle glasses and more hair growing from his nostrils than on his head. "Crazy as a rabid bat. Still alive, last I heard. You should find him out at the Hellman Home."

"Hellman Home?" Danny had asked. "Is that a retirement community?"

The man had laughed, filling the air with the aroma of an overflowing ashtray. "That's one way to put it. Go east past the old Winfield Manor and the fairgrounds. Can't miss it."

And so Danny had gone home, unloaded the groceries, and rounded up Chrissy and the girls.

"We should bring him candy," Liz said.

"I didn't buy any today. Didn't want to give the neighbors the pleasure in case they decide to come back in their costumes."

"Not new candy," Olivia said. "She meant the candy from the purple bag."

Danny felt his guard go up at the thought of giving away the butterscotch candies they had found. "No way!" he shouted. He glared at his girls. Olivia recoiled while tears formed at the edges of Liz's eyes. "Those are ours. We bought this house and everything in it. They don't belong to him."

"Honey, what has gotten over you?" Chrissy asked. "You hate butterscotch. That man was obviously obsessed with them if he went through so much effort to keep them hidden."

"I..." A fog lifted from Danny. "I'm sorry. I don't know what happened there. You're right, we should bring him these candies. We'll get our own to replace them and make use of those little dishes."

Danny opened the cabinet door, retrieved the purple bag, and stood up.

"Are you coming?" Chrissy asked after ushering the girls through the swinging door into the living room. She stood with one foot in each room to hold the door for Danny. His gaze followed his right arm, down to his hand, from which he held the purple bag away from his body as if it contained something rancid or dangerous. It trembled along with his hand.

"Maybe I'll just try one of them. I'm sure he won't remember how many were in here." Danny loosened the drawstring, reached in, and pulled one out. The little golden candy was wrapped in a yellow translucent plastic. *Wellworth's Fine Butterscotch* was printed in red letters. Danny unwrapped it and shoved the candy in his mouth. Sucked on it. Absorbed its flavor. "Not as bad as I remember," he said, then reached in and grabbed another. He tossed it to his wife, who looked at him with doubt but unwrapped it and gave it a chance.

"You're right," Chrissy said, "maybe you need more age and sophistication to appreciate these."

They walked out the front door toward the station wagon, enjoying the sweet hard candies on their tongues. Chrissy stopped in the path to the driveway and held out her hand to stop Danny. He halted and followed her gaze, beyond where the girls waited patiently inside the car.

A crowd stood at the bottom of the driveway. Albie Quentin and his two boys stood among the dozen or so folks that congregated in the street. They didn't move, only stared intently at Chrissy and Danny.

"Good afternoon, folks," Danny called. He tucked the purple sack into the waist at the back of his jeans. "Nice day." He nudged Chrissy to keep walking. She picked up speed, nearly running for the front passenger door. Danny did the same to the driver's side and flicked the power locks as soon as he slammed his door shut.

"They weren't there when we stepped outside," Olivia said. "But as soon as we got in the car, we saw Mr.

Quentin and his boys stop in front of the driveway, then the others all seemed to come out of nowhere."

"Why are they just standing there like that?" Liz asked.

"I don't know, but they're about to get run over if they stay there," Danny said. He started the engine, but it didn't faze the street-side congregants. He put the transmission into drive and inched toward the end of the driveway. Still no movement.

"You can't run them down," Chrissy said.

"Don't worry, I won't." Danny brought the front tires over the sidewalk, down the slight decline into the street. With less than a foot between his sedan and the two Quentin boys, the crowd took a step back in unison. He hit the brakes and took in their faces. "Like zombies," he said.

He let off the brake pedal and drifted forward another foot. Again, the crowd stepped back, synchronized. He continued to push forward, and the towns-people stepped aside one by one until Danny was able to straighten the car out and coast down the street. After the car was twenty feet from the odd ensemble, Danny slammed on the brakes, opened the window, and reached for the sack in the back of his jeans. He held it out the window.

"Honey, what are you doing?" Chrissy asked.

"Just testing a theory." Danny looked in the rearview mirror and took in the faces. They stared at the bag. Hungry. Obsessed. The younger of the Quentin boys was the first to move. He broke out in a sprint toward the car.

"Go, Daddy, go!" Liz shouted from the back seat. The older boy followed his brother, and then the others all ran after the car.

"Please!" Olivia cried.

Danny peeled out, leaving the zombie-like neighbors in a cloud of asphalt dust and smog. He drove to the end of their street and turned onto Main. Raventree Hollow was a fairly small town and the primary business district ran along this street. Pedestrians along the sidewalks all stopped in their tracks, turning to face the Kauers' car as it passed them.

"I get the feeling everyone is watching us," Chrissy said.

"I don't like it," Olivia said. "Not one bit."

"I don't know, kind of feels like we're famous." Everyone turned back to Liz and laughed. The tension broke for the time being as they passed the town's main diner, the flower shop, the barber. Danny thought the only thing missing was a candy shop. Perhaps there had been one some time ago, and that's where the Wellworth's Fine Butterscotch had been purchased from.

An engine revved.

"Daddy, look out!" Olivia shouted. A black muscle car with a gold bird of prey painted on the hood shot out from the parking lot next to the post office and drifted sideways. Danny yanked the wheel to the left, sending the family's car into the wrong lane. There was no oncoming traffic at that moment or else they'd be four more bodies buried at Raventree Memorial Gardens in a few days' time. Instead of braking, Danny sped up and resumed his position in the correct lane, just in front of the muscle car.

"What are you doing? Pull over!" Chrissy shouted. The girls cried in the back seat.

An orange conversion van turned the corner ahead onto Main Street, coming the opposite direction in the next lane. Danny looked over at the passing driver, who stared back with the same expression he had seen on the Quentins and their posse. The van swerved to its right, then swung to its left in a u-turn. The driver hadn't slowed down first, and the van went up on its two right wheels for a few seconds. It went up onto the sidewalk and smashed through a picket fence, mashing the lawn into mud. On its way back to the street, it took out two mailboxes. Danny watched in his rearview mirror as the van took its place in the procession just behind his station wagon and the muscle car.

Danny turned onto the highway in the eastbound lane. His pursuers followed suit, though the van had trouble maintaining its speed and fell behind. The driver of the muscle car had no trouble keeping up and gunned his engine. He rammed the back of the Kauer station wagon, sending the car swerving around the lane, but Danny kept it from entering oncoming traffic in the next lane.

"Just pull over," Chrissy pleaded. "Whatever he wants, just give it to him."

"I can't. I won't let them have it." Danny continued on down the highway. On his left, he spotted a hill with an old but well-maintained mansion at the top, surrounded by a lush garden. "Winfield Manor. The fairgrounds should be next, and then the Hellman Home. We're almost there."

The Kauers took another hit from the muscle car, this time sending them off into the right shoulder. Dirt and rocks sprayed everywhere. Danny corrected course, but he had trouble keeping the car aimed straight.

"Everyone okay?" he asked, though he knew he would continue on no matter their answers. The girls wept from the back seat. Chrissy held onto the handle above her door, crying into her right shoulder.

Another hit. This time from the right side. Danny lost control. His car spun across the divide, into the oncoming lane, and over the other shoulder. A semi-trailer truck heading into Raventree Hollow swerved, narrowly avoiding the Kauer family. It hopped the divide, smashing directly into the muscle car. The muscle car crushed like a can. Just behind it, the conversion van's driver failed to brake in time. If the driver of the smaller car had survived the impact with the big rig, he certainly met his demise when the van smashed into his hot rod from the other end.

Danny ignored the deafening screams of his wife and daughters and the wheezing of his car's engine. He corrected course, passed the fairgrounds, and turned off toward the iron gates of the Hellman Home for Rehabilitation.

Chapter Five

Danny pumped the brakes as he approached a parking stall, but it was no use. The car coasted through the spot until it smashed into the wall of a utility shed. He pulled the emergency brake, bringing the family's journey to a sudden halt.

"Well, we're here."

The girls had stopped screaming. He turned to his wife and locked eyes with her. She said nothing, just stared at him as she struggled to get her breathing under control. Her eyes lowered. She stretched her arm across the center console, picked up the purple bag on Danny's lap, and reached in. She pulled out one of the butterscotch candies.

"If we're going to come this close to death over these things, I at least need to take another one for myself." She unwrapped it and popped the candy into her mouth.

"Can I have one?" Olivia asked.

"Me too." Liz unlatched her seatbelt and jumped off

her booster seat. She reached into the bag and emerged with two candies.

After a few seconds, Liz spit hers onto the ground. Olivia followed suit.

"It's so nasty," Olivia said.

"Tastes like rotten milk," Liz remarked.

Danny and Chrissy looked at each other and laughed.

"Well, these rotten milk candies are sure causing a stir," Danny said. He tucked the bag back into his waistband. "Let's go find out what's so special about them."

They had difficulties with the doors. Danny got his open, but the frame was so mangled that it wouldn't close properly. Chrissy had to turn sideways in her seat and kick her door open. Danny reached into the rear driver's side window and pulled the girls out. With the purple bag in one hand, Danny led his family into the Hellman House.

A nurse stood on the porch with a cigarette. She looked at the foursome in shock as they left their wreck of a vehicle behind and casually approached. Danny waved to her.

"Hello. We're here to see Barry Stetson. We were told he's a resident here." The cigarette dropped from the nurse's lips and fell to the wood planks on the porch. She pointed to the door. Danny nodded to her. "Thank you, ma'am."

Even from the lobby, the place smelled like soiled diapers and rotting meat. The front desk receptionist placed a call to one of the doctors, then hung up. "Mr.

Stetson is allowed visitors at this time. Take the stairs to the third floor, room 314."

"Is he safe to be around?" Chrissy asked. "Do we need any supervision?"

"Oh, Mr. Stetson is quite well-behaved. You'll be just fine with him." The receptionist handed them lanyards with the word *Guest*. The family thanked her and headed toward the stairs.

Gut-wrenching screams and wicked laughter echoed down the halls and reverberated through the stairwell. The stench grew more intolerable as they climbed to the second floor landing, but the third floor provided relief. Danny peaked into a recreation room, where clusters of patients sat around game tables and others lounged alone with magazines. He led the family around a corner and down a corridor until they arrived at room 314.

Danny balled his fingers into a fist, but before he could knock, the door swung open.

"You must be the Kauer family. Come in."

Barry Stetson waddled across the room to a recliner. The family remained at the door for a moment, taking in the space within. It looked like a normal studio apartment, not the padded-walled cell one would expect to see based on any asylum from the movies. Mr. Stetson also looked and sounded perfectly healthy for a man who appeared to be in his eighties.

"Wait," Danny said. "Are you a doctor here? I thought you were here as a patient."

Barry laughed. "If I'm a doctor, I don't know why

I'm paying them to let me stay here. Takes my full pension and then some."

"Sorry, it's just that you seem so normal."

"Well, we're all a little crazy, right? But yes, I am quite a bit healthier than many of the other folks in here."

"If that's the case, why are you here?" Chrissy asked.

"Did you kill someone?" Liz asked.

"No, my dear, though I probably came close to it a time or two." Barry turned to Danny. "Now, where are they? I can smell them."

"Smell who?" Danny asked.

"The butterscotch, you dolt," Barry said. Danny was assured by the gleam in Barry's eyes that the old man was being playful. "I signed the paperwork for the close of escrow. I know you bought my old house. You must have found it."

"We found more than that." Danny pulled the bag out from under his shirt. "We also found a pack of neighbors ready to murder us for these things."

"Exactly why I'm here, locked away from those maniacs. Much safer here."

"Should we not have brought the candies here?" Chrissy asked.

Barry considered the question, then shrugged it off. "They all know I'm here anyway. No matter." He reached for the bag. Danny hesitated, but relented at Chrissy's stare. Barry plucked out a butterscotch. Held it to the light, observing it like a prospector with a nugget of gold. He studied the words on the wrapper as if they contained some coveted wisdom. "Just as I remember it," he said before he unwrapped the butterscotch and inhaled its sweet odor. The satisfaction seemed to take years off of his complexion.

He moaned with delight as he tasted it. "May as well have another," he told the Kauer family. "Go on." Each member of the family reached in and grabbed another candy. Even though they had spit theirs out only minutes earlier, the kids didn't hesitate to try it again, entranced by the old man's apparent love for the stuff.

"Blech," Liz exclaimed as she spit hers back into the wrapper. "Why do people like these so much?"

"That's what I asked myself many years ago," Barry said. The candy in his mouth was still intact, but he reached in for another one anyway. He popped it into his mouth and managed to talk with both candies at his cheeks like a squirrel carrying multiple acorns. He reached over to an end table next to his recliner and lifted an amber candy dish, identical to the ones back at the house. He held it out to the kids. "Try these instead. More your style, I bet."

The girls each took two small chocolates with glee.

"Butterscotch is a taste for a different generation, I guess," Barry went on. "In my day, the kids couldn't get enough of the stuff. I have four boys of my own, and they have a few kids each. Even some great-grandchildren out there somewhere, but they don't visit or write. I've lost track of how many there are. Back when my kids were young, we had candy dishes everywhere. This was before dentists discouraged us from eating too many sweets. Candy was around so often, it didn't even tempt anyone. Reach over and grab one when you're idle. Offer it to company. That sort of thing. Not a big deal at all. We had chocolates like these sometimes, but more often it was hard candy.

"The strawberry ones," Chrissy said.

"And the coffee flavor," Danny added.

"The very ones, yes. And then," Barry gestured toward the purple sack, "there were the butterscotch candies. Kids usually despised them, which left more for the adults. Maybe that was the point. Let the kids have the chocolates and strawberries while us old folks utilized our refined palates with the butterscotch.

"My kids weren't like other children, though. One day they decided that they loved butterscotch. They snatched every last one out of the dishes in the family room, the living room, the dining room, the kitchen. Even the backups in the pantry. No big deal, I thought, I'll just buy more of those than the other kinds. I didn't really worry until their teeth started to rot from all the cavities. It's normal for kids to get some cavities, but every single tooth seemed to decay on my boys. I stopped buying candy for quite some time. Then they all got their adult teeth, grew up, went out on their own. That's when I started buying it again. Making use of my little dishes, offering sweets to my guests and neighbors.

"And then the grandkids came along.

"Once again I could no longer leave that candy out. Those greedy little monsters would dump entire bowls into their pockets. I yelled at their daddies who told me I was being ridiculous. Anytime my family visited, they cleaned me out of every last piece. Eventually I had enough."

"You killed them all?" Olivia asked.

"Worse. I used a spell."

The room went silent for a moment, and then Liz chuckled. "Like a witch!" she exclaimed. "Like a fairy tale."

Danny and Chrissy looked at each other, unsure how to react to Mr. Stetson's claims.

"Not so far off, actually," Barry said. He pointed out the window. Danny followed the direction of the old man's finger. Across the neighboring fairgrounds was the hill with the mansion on top. "You see, I went to an estate sale up there after old Philip Winfield croaked. He had nobody left in his family line, so his lawyers were selling off the goods to the townsfolk. Fancy things at dirt-cheap prices. The whole town upgraded the decor in their homes for pennies on the dollar over the course of a weekend. I was late, having worked throughout the weekend at the car dealership I managed at the time. By the time I got to Winfield Manor that Sunday evening, it was slim pickings. Down in the basement, there were some water-logged books. I sorted through them under the dim light of the lantern I was provided. The lighting wasn't so great deep below the house and I hadn't even gone too far down the winding corridors under there. Some of the books were truly ancient, probably came over from whatever part of Europe the family line descended from. Those weren't written in English. Couldn't tell you what languages they were.

"I finally found an armful with words I could recognize. Thought they'd look nice on my shelves, make me look sophisticated and all. I hauled them up the cellar stairs to the kitchen where I could actually read them, and just like this little girl said, it was the stuff of fairy tales. Witchcraft. Spells. Magic. Whatever you want to call it.

"I looked around nervously to make sure nobody was watching. I knew whatever I had was uncouth, if you catch my drift. Pagan symbols, maybe Satanist. I'm not sure, I just know that I felt like a kid breaking all his parents' rules. I opened the cover, and it felt like a cold wind had blown out from the book and enveloped me. I heard voices. It was the managers of the estate sale closing up the house for the night. I slammed that book shut, left the others right on the table, and paid them for the one book.

"Back at home, I closed all the curtains, locked the doors. That feeling of being a naughty child never left me as I flipped through those pages. The house grew frigid, so I cranked up the heat, but it didn't seem to be enough. I got a good fire going in the fireplace—not something I did often because the kids had asthma years before—and sat beside it to continue reading. That's when I found it."

Barry Stetson grew quiet. He stared off into the wall, as if watching his own memories projected in front of him. Danny looked to his wife and arched a brow. Chrissy shrugged back at him. The girls leaned forward in their own chairs, engrossed in the pause just as much as the story.

"Sorry," Barry said, shaking out of his daze. "I'm trying to remember exactly what was running through my mind at that time. Why I thought there was such desperation over those damn candies. Yet that's all I could think about as I read this particular passage. You see, it was a spell of possession. Protecting an item of great value to ensure others won't take it from you.

"I recited the incantation written on those pages. I followed the steps: drops of blood from my palm in a dish"—Barry lifted his left hand, revealing an old scar across the palm—"and the item to be protected, some hair from my head, and some other things. All to be thrown in the flames, then retrieved after half a minute. To my surprise, the candy dish I used was fully intact when I managed to get it out of the fireplace. The candies weren't even melted.

"I thought I was keeping others from coveting the butterscotch, but in the end, it did the exact opposite. My oldest son was due the next afternoon for lunch with his wife and kids. That was the first time I realized the spell hadn't worked as planned. Things got physical. My son was like a madman, tearing apart the pantry looking for those candies. I thought his wife would calm him, but she was on her own hunt through the house, looking under beds and in closets. Their kids, too. It was like they were zombies on the hunt for brains to consume. That's when I stopped inviting my family over. Friends and neighbors stopped by from time to time, but as soon as they stepped through the front door, a switch flipped inside of them and they went on the hunt for my butterscotch. The only company I had was the cats. They weren't mine. Just showed up on my doorstep, one after another. I wasn't threatened by them because I could tell they were there to help guard the butterscotch. But they weren't enough.

"I revisited the book one desperate night. That's when I found the other spell." Barry reached for the purple bag and tugged it from Danny's lap. He turned it upside down, dumping the contents onto his own lap. A single piece fell out. "Is this it?"

"I suppose we ate all the rest on the way and as we talked with you here," Danny replied. Barry held the final piece up in front of his face, again viewing it as an immensely valuable item.

"Just as well," Barry said. "The time had to come, sooner or later."

"What was the other spell for?" Olivia asked.

"It was supposed to scare off anyone from wanting to take the last of my butterscotch candies. Again, I was very desperate. Not in my right mind. Everyone wanted to raid my candy supply, and they all turned into absolute maniacs anytime they were around me. I could hardly go out to the supermarket without getting mobbed by those weirdos. I couldn't take it anymore.

"I recited the words, did a fairly similar routine. When it was done, I didn't feel like anything was different at first. Not until I ate another piece of butterscotch. That's when I felt it, like a clock ticking toward its alarm. Each piece of candy was another second of the countdown. When I got down to the last handful, I couldn't take it anymore. I had to get away from it all.

That's when I checked myself into this place. For my own safety, and for everyone else's."

"And what happens when the clock's count is down to zero?" Fear seeped into Chrissy's voice. She pointed at the butterscotch in Barry Stetson's grasp. "What happens when that last piece is gone?"

Barry's look of bewilderment turned to a smile. "The world will end, that's all."

Silence. Danny studied the man, trying to understand the humor. Attempting to decipher some kind of morality lesson from the story. It was clearly fictional, he thought. There were no spells. Magic wasn't real. Witchcraft, as his daughter had said, was a thing of fairy tales. He broke the silence with nervous laughter.

"Good one, Mr. Stetson. You know, you really had us there." Danny reached over and patted Olivia on the knees. She turned to her little sister, who was as confused as the rest of them. The story Barry told had seemed so real, and yet...

Barry grasped one end of the twisty wrapper between his left pointer finger and thumb. He did the same with his other hand on the opposite side. He pulled at the cellophane. The candy twisted in its wrapper, then fell into Barry's right palm.

"Here goes nothing," the old man said. He popped the butterscotch into his mouth.

The family sat there, watching him suck on the hard candy, savoring its taste.

Barry grunted. Reached up and rested a hand on his cheek. His expression of delight turned into one of shock. Of horror. He gasped for air. Fell out of his chair.

His head hit the ground. The family stared as the man died in front of them.

His lips twitched into a smile. His eyes opened as he sat up.

"Just playing with you all," Barry said. "There's nothing magical about it. That old book didn't work. You see, it was all in my head. All it did was make me paranoid."

A collective sigh of relief spread across the room. Danny stood up and walked to the window, taking in the view.

Behind him, he heard a crunch as Mr. Stetson bit down on the last of his butterscotch. The old man swallowed.

They all laughed together.

It would all be okay.

And then the fire fell from the sky.

A MACHETE & QUILL HORROR
RYAN HOYT
THE
HOARDER'S
HOUSE
A RAVENTREE HOLLOW STORY

Preface

Parts of this story are based on actual events.

Okay, I'm sure you can figure out which parts are definitely *not* real, but there are some elements that are based on some sad truths.

I've wanted to write this story for years. It's lived in my head pretty much as you'll read it here. Trauma wanting to tell a story. Horror making it possible. After all, isn't that what horror is best at? A way to process our pain and fears. An outlet for the darker thoughts that hide in the corners of our brains. A way to turn sadness into revenge in a safe way that hurts nothing but the trees (if you're reading this on paper, I guess).

Anyways, go put on some work boots. Get your tetanus shot. Grab a gas mask and maybe even an air freshener. You may want all of it for this story.

The Hoarder's House

"It's my childhood home," Erica scoffed from the passenger seat. "Of course we have to do this."

Alan flicked the right blinker on and moved to the slow lane, allowing an aggressive raised pickup to pass him. "I get it, but I still think we should just hire a junk removal company to clear the place out. The storage unit is going to get expensive."

"We're probably going to need to toss most of it anyways, but there are a lot of memories in that house. Besides, my sister may still show up. She wouldn't be happy if we tossed her things."

Alan grimaced. "There are probably going to be fleas or mites on everything. I don't even want to know."

They continued on a desolate stretch of highway for three hours, mostly in silence. Four weeks prior, Erica had received the call from her sister Linda's human resources representative. Linda hadn't arrived for work in three days, had no vacation request in the system, and didn't even call to report she was sick. Linda's phone went straight to voicemail, and her texts remained unread. Erica phoned a couple of Linda's elderly neighbors whose landlines still existed, some of the only phone numbers she could recall from her youth in the days before cell phones.

The police hadn't been too concerned at first. Since Linda was not a minor and had no history of mental illness on record, they were slow to process the missing person report. Outside of a couple attempted wellness checks—knocking on the door for a few minutes, receiving no reply, then leaving—they couldn't be bothered to do much more. By the end of week three, they finally admitted it was a curious situation, and told Erica she may want to come and take care of the house. The neighbors had complained about smells, though the officers were clear it was not the stench of a decaying human body. Those words did little to ease Erica's worries.

At the start of week four, the school year ended. Erica submitted her students' grades at the earliest opportunity and Alan used up a couple days of his vacation stockpile. They got into the car and made the trek to Erica's hometown, a place she normally chose to avoid at all costs. She had been so adamant about going that Alan realized it was more serious than he and the police had originally given credit for. Linda was certainly dead or gone. Something had to be done about the house. The plan was to clean the whole place out, take stock of the needed repairs and upgrades, hire a contractor and real estate agent, and let the professionals get it ready and listed on the market.

The only problem was the way Linda had kept it.

Linda had occupied the house ever since their parents' passing in a car accident fourteen years prior. She'd been in a nearby apartment before that, and Erica had moved out of state, so it made sense that Linda would move in despite their parents leaving it to both sisters in their will. Erica and Alan had visited only once, two years after the funeral. If the state of the place then was any indication, Alan's stomach turned at the thought of it now. They'd tried to visit a couple more times over the years, but Linda hadn't let them inside. She'd insisted that the couple stay in a hotel downtown, and she would meet them anywhere except the house. The couple didn't even need to ask why.

Now, as they pulled up in front of the house, the sickness in Alan's stomach intensified. His wife had gone pale at the sight of it. Alan reached over and wiped a tear from her cheek. She flinched at his touch, then turned to him. "Linda wasn't always like this. I think losing my parents was too much for her."

They got out of the car with hesitation and stood together on the sidewalk, observing the front yard. The weeds had been growing for far longer than Linda's four-week disappearance. The thorny ones had sprouted up to Alan's shoulders, and he was no small man. From the glow of the streetlights, random trash sparkled like silver throughout the thick overgrowth. A couple windows overlooking the yard had been covered with plywood, which appeared bloated from moisture. The stench of rot seemed to come from what had once been a luscious lawn, and Alan was certain it'd be just as bad inside. Erica whimpered.

"Are you sure you want to do this?" Alan asked.

"No." She stepped forward anyways down the path, walled in like some kind of secret garden. She pulled her keys from the purse as she went, fumbling through them until she found the one she hadn't used in over a decade. Without a moment's hesitation, she put the key in the deadbolt lock. It turned with a resounding click and Erica twisted the knob.

As Alan had feared, a wave of foul odor greeted them, seeping through the opening front door like a freediver gasping for air at his reemergence from the deep. He stepped back and gagged, nearly twisting his ankle as he teetered off the porch step and landed awkwardly. He was impressed at Erica's strong stomach, as she didn't even flinch at the smell. It had a sharpness under the musk. Sour. Rot and decay. Beefy sewage. Alan tried to describe it to himself in all those terms but no single label accurately defined the complex and horrendous olfactory offense that emanated from the depths of the house.

He watched Erica step into the dark foyer and reach for the light switch. This was the house she'd grown up in. She knew its features well. Even so, she had not been prepared for what was illuminated by the harsh bulb in the front hall.

The entryway was filled, barely allowing for the arc of the door's path to open and close. Alan vaguely recalled from his one visit here that the entry tiles had been a pale cream color. Now, they were caked in a dozen years of dirt and crumbs and hair. He squinted at what he was sure was movement among the grimy floor, what he had mistaken for specks of dirt were other things entirely. Mites or fleas or tiny ants, living large off the mess provided to them.

Beyond the bare patch of floor at the entrance, the piles began, stretching out as far as he could see in the house. Discarded shirts, winter coats, unopened junk mail, torn up envelopes, magazines, bubble wrap. Shoes jutted out of the piles with not a single match in sight. Winter gloves scattered about. A broom handle poked upward like a flagpole, a bra dangling from the tip. Alan bent over the pile of junk in front of him and brushed the bra off.

"May as well start the cleaning right here." He pulled the broom handle out of the mess only to find the other end of the shaft snapped off and jagged. "Or not," he said as he tossed it aside. "It may come in handy later, though. Who knows what lurks in this dump."

Erica's silence spoke volumes. His humor and sarcasm were not appreciated right now. He opened his mouth to apologize, but she waved him off. "Let's start in the kitchen," she suggested. "Maybe that's where most of the smell is coming from."

Alan held his arms out in the direction of the kitchen. "After you, dear."

Erica lifted her right leg and stepped up on the knee-high pile of rubbish. She put her weight on that foot to propel herself up, but stumbled as the pile gave way. Alan reached out to catch her, pivoting awkwardly to lean over the mess. Erica wasn't large by any stretch, yet the angle and the force of her collapse caused something to pop in Alan's back. He groaned. "Sorry," Erica whispered, then pulled herself back up and onto the pile. This time it held firm. She reached one hand up to the ceiling and the other to the wall to keep steady.

Alan followed suit, but lifting his leg sent shooting pains up his spine. He pushed through it, taking one step, then a second. A rumble stopped him in his tracks. "Did you feel that?"

"It's just the junk under our weight," Erica said. She smirked at him. "You scared, tough guy?"

"Maybe of tetanus. Should have got our shots before coming in here."

The foyer split in two directions. Most of the living space including the kitchen was upstairs, while a spare bedroom suite and sitting room took up the lower level, with the foyer just in between the two. Erica started her ascent, and it was a true climb up the unstable mound of junk.

"It's a mental illness," Erica said in anticipation of Alan's comments about her sister. "She can't help it."

Once she made it to the top, Alan began his own climb. As he neared the landing, the rubble quaked again. A pile of old CDs tipped off the top and slid down toward Alan. A basketball rolled after them. Alan attempted to dodge the items but the flailing of his limbs just perpetuated the avalanche. Detritus under him made its descent, bringing Alan down with it.

"Oh, honey!" Erica called.

"I'm alright." Alan lay sprawled on his back on the foyer pile, his progress demolished in one fell swoop.

"At least the stairs are cleared off," Erica pointed out. Alan struggled his way upright and saw what she was talking about. The trash slide had brought the bulk of the mess down where he'd landed. Now that the steps were cleared off, the carpet came into view for the first time. From his vantage point just inches from them, he could make out more of the movement he'd seen earlier. Fleas bounced around on each step. Much thicker than those critters were the rat turds.

"We may want to get checked for ringworm after this," he said. "And rabies." He got up onto the steps and climbed with more ease than before. Erica held a hand out for him from the top landing, which he accepted despite the pain in his back. At the top, he heard a thud.

"It sounds like it came from the lower level," Erica said.

"It took a hell of an effort just getting up here. I'm not going back down just yet."

"We can check it out later. Probably just the junk rolling the rest of the way down to that level. Let's get to the kitchen."

Erica led the way, nearly tripping over the remains of a vacuum cleaner. When they reached the kitchen, Alan's stomach lurched. He fumbled around for a receptacle. He found an open chip bag and brought it to his face. A small rat emerged from within and brushed against his cheek as it leapt away. Alan filled the bag with vomit.

"Oh, Linda," Erica cried out at the state of the kitchen. As she said the words, there was another rumble under their feet. Another thud sounded out downstairs as if to answer.

The kitchen looked just like the rest of the house, only the trash was a mixture of decomposing food waste, discarded wrappers, and a seemingly endless supply of soiled dishes and cookware. Every inch of the countertops and stove were covered with detritus. Flies circled the room like vultures over a pack of dead horse carcasses. Maggots crawled on top of each other in a scramble to get to the most rotted parts of the food scraps.

And then there was the sink.

The soupy liquid that filled the kitchen sink was reddish brown with chunks of soggy lettuce, soaked crusts of bread, and bits of plastic packaging. Underneath the rotten smells, Alan caught a whiff of tomato sauce and garlic, like a tomato bisque had been discarded as the last straw before the sink decided to give up the ghost and clog itself. In a rhythmic fashion, the drain gurgled about once every three seconds, sending a sludgy bubble up with each belch. Alan opened the chip bag and puked a second time.

"Linda lived in this," Erica said. The sadness in her voice broke Alan's heart. "For over a decade, she lived in this. What kind of sister am I to have let this go on for so long?"

"You tried. You wanted to intervene much earlier, but she wouldn't let you. Like you said, it's a mental illness. Linda—"

Another rumble among the junk.

"—is not—"

Another sound from downstairs.

"—right in the head. You did hear that, didn't you?"

Erica nodded, her eyes wide with fear. "I think she's down there." She pushed past Alan and back toward the hall. "Linda, are you here? It's Erica and Alan. We want to help you. Lin?" Another quake rocked the house, shaking the continuous trash pile like a tray of jello.

"Honey, wait," Alan said as he grabbed her wrist. "This doesn't feel right. Even if Linda is here, we don't know how her mental state will be."

Erica shook out of his grasp. "That's my sister, not a monster. She's not going to hurt me." Alan didn't agree but he let her go.

"I'll check the other rooms," Alan said. Erica only nodded as she climbed her way back to the stairs. Alan started to turn away from the kitchen when he heard a tapping sound. Coagulated grease dripped downward from the vent above the cooktop range, hanging like a thick strand of snot before succumbing to its own weight and landing on one of the burners with a plop. Another tapping came from the vent just before the metal filter popped out of place and crashed down on the stove, with two well-fed rats plummeting down with it. One hopped from the range, landed on all fours on the grimy linoleum, and skittered behind the refrigerator. The other dove into the murky contents of the sink. Three small bubbles rose to the surface, but the rat did not return for fresh air.

Alan maneuvered his way to the sink and flipped a

switch. The garbage disposal whirred softly, not the usual throaty mechanical snarl one might expect. The blades were caught on debris that had been wedged down the drain for who knew how long. Something shifted in the depths of the sink or farther into the drain, perhaps the rat attempting to fight its way out. It seemed to have kicked loose whatever had clogged the disposal. The blades spun, slow at first, then with growing intensity, the chopping and slicing sounds increasing in brutality. Clouds of all different colors puffed through the demented soup.

The blades stopped, the entire system muting at once. The next noise to come out was indisputably that of a person screaming under water, muffled, A smattering of bubbles accompanied it. Rather than popping, the bubbles sat at the surface and grew in size. When they were each the size of an overturned cereal bowl, Alan bent over the sink, his head cocked so his right ear hovered eight inches above the mixture. He couldn't make out what was being screamed or whose voice it was.

Pop!

The bubbles burst at once, spewing sludge onto his face. He flinched at the contact and made to stand straight, but his injured back would not comply. The pain caused him to buckle at the knees, his head falling toward the mixture in the sink. The blades began to spin at full force once again, spraying the nasty stuff into his mouth and nostrils. He tried again to push away from it, but something grabbed hold of his head. He reached for what felt like a creature's writhing tentacles, pulling him toward the sludge. It wanted to suck him into garbage disposal.

It tightened its grip, and he tightened his. Frantic, his eyes darted around the junk piled on the counter-tops. A serrated knife sat on a stained cutting board. He reached for it. It was rusty, but hopefully still sharp enough. He had just enough clearance between his head and the top of the sink's contents to reach the serpen-tine *thing* that kept its tight grip on him. He hacked at it, then sawed with the serrated edges. It loosened and he pulled away from it. As it retracted into the murky depths of the sink, Alan thought it looked like nothing more than overly long spaghetti noodles wrapped tenfold around each other to form a strong vine. And then it was gone. The sink's contents lessened as the disposal sliced and diced until finally the sink was empty. Alan flipped the switch, bringing silence back to the kitchen. After a few deep breaths, he moved on.

The living room was more of the same. Piles of clothing, food wrappers, various sorts of packaging, and miscellaneous electronic gadgets, chargers, and cables covered the floor and buried the couch. The hallway to the bedrooms didn't break the pattern, nor did the two guest bedrooms. The hall bathroom's toilet, sink, and tub were all backed up, sewage filling to the rims and overflowing onto the floor in a brown pool like some toxic rendition of Niagra Falls. The last door at the end of the hall was the master bedroom.

Certainly this one room of all of them will be in decent shape, he thought, as his sister-in-law had to sleep some-where. He pushed the door open and found that he was mostly right. The sheets let off a stink of their own from lack of washing for what must have been years. Sweat and skin flakes had given the sheets a crusty, grimy look with an unsettling sheen. A mouse sprawled out dead on one of the pillows like a bow on a beautifully wrapped present. Other than a clear lack of laundering and vacuuming, and of course the deceased rodent, this one room looked almost alright.

Alan turned to check on the in-suite bathroom when a thought crossed his mind. Erica had walked away from him five minutes earlier. The house hadn't quaked since then. There had been no more strange sounds from downstairs. Had she found Linda?

"Erica?" Alan called, rushing to the hallway. "Is she down there? Did you find her?"

No answer. Alan quickened his pace, leaping over a protruding pile, but his back shot out pain as he landed, knocking him off his feet. He rolled over in the detritus, attempting to push himself up, but his body did not comply. A crinkling sound near his head made him flinch, sending more pain up to his shoulders and neck. He saw a flash of white approach his face. Before he could swat it away, it wrapped over his head. He reached for it, understanding by touch what it was. The plastic grocery bag tightened. He took in a breath before a scream, but the plastic pulled taut at his nostrils and mouth. No air reached his lungs.

Alan's hands worked their way frantically all around the bag. He expected to feel his attacker holding the bag against him, but there was nobody manipulating it. No hands to pry off of him. He pinched at the plastic and pulled, stretching it until a hole opened up over his face. He yanked the rest of the plastic off and gasped for oxygen, grateful for it even despite the stink that tainted it.

He ignored the pain as best he could, crawling toward the stairs. Whatever was happening in his spine did not allow him to stand, so he slid down the stairs on his belly like a child on a waterslide. On the foyer landing, he retrieved the broken broomstick, its blunt edge making it like a spear. The piles of trash hiding the stairs down to the lower level were even thicker than anything above—this must have been the original dumping ground for Linda; even the stink was worse here, a more aged and decayed quality to it. His descent was even less graceful than on the first flight of stairs, and he tumbled and somersaulted down, slamming into the closed door at the bottom.

A whole new pain filled him then. The jagged broomstick had lodged into the flesh of his belly during the fall. He gripped it with both hands, took a ragged breath, then yanked it out. His scream would have been piercing anywhere else, but the immense amount of trash and debris around the house absorbed the sound waves.

He tossed the bloody object aside and listened. No sounds came from the other side of the door. Not even breathing, despite his wife having come down here just minutes earlier. Fear overtook Alan as his hand found the knob. He turned it and pushed the door open.

Vomit. Raw sewage. Rotten eggs. Stale piss. Trash baking in the sun. Spoiled fish. No foul smell that came to mind could compare in the slightest to what penetrated his nostrils when that door opened. Dizziness fell upon him along with an intense desire to evacuate his bowels and stomach and bladder all at once. He may have actually done one or all of those things, but he didn't know in his present state. His mind was somewhere else as he took in the sight.

The junk towered from floor to ceiling. Mixed in with everything he'd already seen throughout the house of horrors, there was also rotting vegetation, liquifying in some late stage of decay, coupled with carcasses of neighborhood cats and squirrels and birds, maggots protruding from sunken eye sockets and out of stiff gaping mouths.

And then there was the pair of eyes.

Alan had met Linda a few times over the years, but not as often as one would think a brother- and sister-in-law would see each other. The present situation was a clear indication of why the woman had distanced herself all this time. Still, he'd seen her enough to note just how strikingly similar her emerald green eyes were to Erica's. Those were the eyes he was staring at now, only they weren't in her head. They were nearly at the same level of Alan's own eyes as he was on his hands and knees at the room's entrance. One was wedged into the pages of a rolled-up magazine, the other a few inches away and slightly higher than the first, wrapped in a dirty sock. Even though they were disconnected from wherever Linda's body was, there was still life in them. They moved in unison, studying the newcomer.

The pile shifted. Alan didn't know if this *thing* with

his sister-in-law's eyes recognized him. As the heap moved, it morphed into a shape vaguely resembling something he'd expected to see from an ancient religion. It had many arms, if you could call them that, made up of discarded towels and soiled clothing items, cardboard wrapping paper rolls, and even a garden hose.

"Where's Erica?" Alan demanded of the creature. "Where is my wife?"

The thing shifted, cocking its head as if in some vague understanding. Perhaps the name *Erica* rang a bell to some part of Linda's subconscious that may have still existed somewhere within.

A sound came out from within its depths. Muffled, but unmistakably Erica. "Get help," he thought she said. "Run!"

"Erica!" Alan pushed himself up, ignoring the explosions of pain across his back. He used the full weight of his body to slam into the mass and push inside of it. He reached his arms through despite not being able to see beyond the outer layer. She was in there somewhere. He knew it.

Another sound came from the beast as Alan pulled his arms out one at a time, fistfuls of debris dug out. He would tunnel his way toward her if he had to.

The hose slithered around his torso three times before he felt it in all its rage. It tightened, knocking the wind from him and sending more pain through his spine, up his shoulders, into the back of his head.

"Let her go, damn it! She is your sister! She's my wife!"

The tightening ceased and the creature shifted.

Something that sounded like airy flatulence released from the depths, then morphed into what resembled a hoarse voice. "Sssssisssterrr... My... Mine. My sssissssssterrrrr..."

"Yes, Linda, she's your—" his words turned to a scream as the hose tightened again.

"My sssssisssssterrrr."

"Don't hurt her, you bitch! Aaah! Let her go. Let me go. We only wanted to help you."

The two eyeballs popped out from the depths of the trash heap, only inches from Alan's own eyes.

"Let her go? Mine. My sssssissssterrrr. Here. Forever."

Alan whimpered in pain. He kicked at the monster, but it had no effect. "Don't do it. Please, you're better than this. And I love her. I'm your brother-in-law. Don't you remember?"

"My... brotherrrrrrrr?" It regarded him with those discarded eyes, turning him around and studying him from all sides like a jeweler with a rare diamond. "My... Mine."

The detritus shifted in the creature's bulk, a hole opening up. The stench intensified. The hose tightened, snapping Alan in two at his stomach, and before the pain completely overtook his senses, he saw himself being swallowed up.

His screams faded quickly. The creature's makeshift limbs fell to the ground, blending in with the rest of the trash. The eyes rolled back into the pile, which came to rest on the ground of the lower level of the hoarder's house.

FREDDY GOODMAN

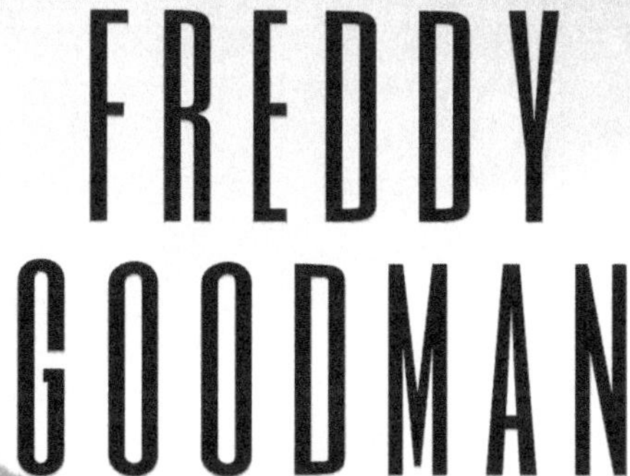

Preface

I've often wondered if Teddy Duchamp (from Stephen King's *The Body* and the film adaptation *Stand By Me*) and other characters like him in my favorite coming-of-age stories and films would have really changed as they grew older.

If so, what would have been the catalyst for that change?

How long would it have taken?

What would be done with a new lease on life?

I wanted to explore that idea with this character I named Freddy Goodman. It's a little derivative and a bit of an homage, but that's by design.

As a side note, this story is not really horror. Hey, if Stephen King can insert non-horror coming-of-age stories like *The Body* into his collections, I can too, right?

I hope you enjoy this story. Thanks for reading.

Chapter One

"Freddy Goodman showing up for his own wedding?" The chatter flowed in through the after-hours cash window of the Avery Fill-R-Up station all the way from the pumps. "I'll believe it when my dead mother—Lord rest her soul—shows up for Gracie's birthday party, funeral gown and all."

The laughter stabbed into my ears as I handed change over the counter to Mariah Hawthorne. She took the coins in her left hand but brought her right hand up to pat my inked and scarred forearm.

"Don't you go try to fight them, Freddy," Mariah said. "Not this time. You know Sheriff Hoskins will gladly lock you up again, wedding day or not. Deep breaths now, boy."

I stared at the old woman but did not comply with the breathing exercise. I don't know what she saw in my eyes, but her hopeful look soured. She shook her head in disappointment and hobbled out to her car, carton of menthols in one hand, cane in the other.

I shifted my glance to Tommy Bloom and Jacob Farmer, fueling up their pickups at the same time as if they had coordinated. They hadn't changed much in the twenty years since high school. Same black baseball caps, black t-shirts, and shorts down nearly to their ankles. The beer guts were newer, but the same could be said for everyone still stuck in Tower Falls from the class of 2001, which is just about everybody except my three best friends. Could I even call them *best friends* when we lost touch after graduation? Was I ever even that close to them to begin with?

"I'm not paying you to daydream, Goodman."

The boss's voice shook me out of my daze. I reached for the rag I kept next to the register and started to wipe the counter. I had all sorts of tricks to look busy in moments like those, but Mr. Avery saw right through them.

"Sorry, sir. What are you doing in so early?"

"Boy, it's your wedding day. You know what they're saying the odds are that you won't show up tonight? I had to place my bet in your favor, being that I have at least some control over you. You better be there now that my wallet is counting on it. I'm covering the rest of your shift so you can get on home and shower for once. Put on something nice so you don't arrive in your work shirt, name tag and all."

I didn't need a written invitation. I nodded to Mr. Avery and made my way around the counter and out the door. Tommy and Jacob were still there, pulling a couple light beers out of a cooler from the back of Tommy's pickup. Jacob flipped me the bird while Tommy held out his can.

"How 'bout a sip before your big no-show tonight?" Tommy called to me. I ignored him and walked around to the back of the station where my car was parked. I could still hear them laughing and chanting "Freddy Goodman ain't no good man" as if it was still funny after high school. And middle school. And grade school. My old man told me he heard the same line when he was a kid, and his pappy before him. That's Tower Falls for you.

Then again, I wasn't much of a good man. Nor was my dad. I heard my grandpa wasn't anything to write home about either, but he died in a blaze of gunfire long before I was ever born. He tried to knock over a gas station. This gas station, in fact.

I got my key in the door of my rusted old LeBaron, but something caught my eye before I pulled the handle. Just beyond the gravel lot behind the gas station, where Mr. Avery has me park my old beater among the dumpsters and the rest of the trash, the forest begins. There are a couple miles of woods before the mountains rise up, the mountains where *she* lives. But I'll tell you about her later. There were critters jutting in and out from the edge of the forest, popping around like they were in a game of Whack-A-Mole down at the Penny Lanes Bowling Alley.

I left the keys hanging out of the car door and went in for a closer look. Not *too* close, mind you; I hadn't been inside those woods for twenty-five years, and I planned to keep it that way. But then I saw what they were. Not just any creatures. They were cats.

Her cats.

I don't know how long those feline fleabags live, so maybe these weren't the same ones my friends and I followed all those years ago, the cats that led us to that witch. They looked the same, though, including the ones we called One-Eyed Willy and Ringworm Patch. Dead-on identical if not the same cats still breathing after more than two decades. I kicked some gravel towards them—nothing violent, I'm not as deranged as people in town like to think (*Freddy Goodman ain't no good man*)—and walked back to my car.

That's when their chorus of meows began. I got my hands on my keys in the door before turning around once more. I've never been good with numbers, but I guessed there were thirty of those cats standing at the edge of the tree line.

Something dug into the back of my neck. I turned to find One-Eyed Willy perched on the rust-spotted roof of the LeBaron, one paw up, ready to claw out my eyes. Make us kindred spirits, I guess. An eye for an eye or whatever. I suppose it was my rock that did that to him, but I was just a stupid twelve-year-old kid back then. Last thing I needed was to show up to my wedding later that evening wearing a fresh eye-patch.

My wedding! I glanced down at my watch. Noon, almost on the dot. I still had a good eight hours. We planned to just have something simple and cheap. I don't have any family around anymore. Lizzie still has her mother and two sisters, so they're of course coming, no matter how much they hate my guts. A few of her friends, too. I got none of those, so it's going to be quite uneven. Wouldn't surprise me if a few random spectators show up uninvited just to watch me make an ass of myself one way or another. Lizzie kept telling me to invite my old friends, the Tower Falls escape artists, but I told her once you leave the Falls, you don't come back for no reason whatsoever. Why bother? Anyway, it was going to be a simple affair down at the chapel that neither of us actually attend on Sundays, a quick reception in the fellowship hall with some late evening desserts, and I promised Lizzie I'd partake in none of the alcohol. Last thing she needs from me on our wedding night is another one of my drunken episodes and a visit from Sheriff Hoskins.

Before I knew it, the cats had surrounded the car. Their meowing didn't let up. Maybe they were just starving, but something told me it was more than that. They were trying to draw me into that forest. Peer pressure or something. And if there's one thing anyone in Tower Falls knows about ol' Freddy Goodman, he can be pressured into just about anything, no matter how stupid.

Eight hours was plenty of time.

I left the keys hanging in the door and walked through that front line of trees for the first time in a quarter of a century.

Towards *her*.

Chapter Two

The awe and wonder about this place that filled me as a kid wasn't present anymore. Maybe back then there wasn't all this trash gathering among the trees. Chip bags, beer cans, used contraceptive devices, discarded needles, an old transmission. I even found the burnt husk of an import from the eighties—maybe the same year as the car my mama handed down to me. No, there was nothing majestic about these woods unless tetanus really excites you.

It was after the fourth or fifth broken bottle I crunched over that I needed to stop and pull glass from the soles of my shoes. I lost the cats, but I knew where they were heading. A couple hundred feet deeper into the woods, the trash thinned out and the overgrowth thickened. There weren't any clear trails through this part of the woods when I was a kid, nor would there be now, but the only directions that mattered were toward the mountain or away from the mountain.

It sounded simpler than it was.

Once the sounds of the two-lane highway disappeared and the trees really started growing closer together, I couldn't even see the mountains through them. It was half past noon, but the canopy blocked out most of the light. I thought I was going in a straight line, but I had to veer around shrubs and fallen branches enough that I couldn't quite tell anymore which direction I was headed in. It was then I realized that I had left my phone back at the station under the counter. I wasn't expecting to hear from Lizzie before the wedding ceremony anyways—she wanted to follow that tradition of not seeing or speaking to each other leading up to it—but I could have made use of that map application. Maybe I *would* be late for my own wedding after all. *Freddy Goodman ain't no good man.*

My eyes were following a complex series of webs constructed among the trees a few feet above my head when I tripped over a large rock. I threw my hands out to catch my fall, but it didn't matter. I was at the edge of a rocky hill, and I was going to roll. The tumble took me over many more stones jutting out. I lifted my head just out of the way of one of them, but a tree stump rushed right into my field of vision and directly into my face before I could react.

I don't know how long I was sprawled out on the ground. When my eyes opened again, an orange cat was licking blood off of my cheek. I reached up to wipe the crimson, only to find a gash three inches long. I stroked the bridge of my nose, but it seemed to be crooked in the same places it had been since Kenny Slattery bashed that barstool into it seven or eight years back. I had that one coming, though. I was stealing credit card numbers from the tab file behind the bar. *Ain't no good man* and all that.

I sat up and saw a light show, but there didn't seem to be any serious concussion—I've had a few of those as well. A dozen of the cats backed away as I rose. They must have come back for me while I was out cold. Seriously, how long was it? I glanced at my watch, only to find it had been shattered. It was just a cheap Casio, but I've had it as long as I can remember. Again I was starting to fear that I'd be late for my big night, but I was determined to press on. These cats would be leading me back to *her*, and there had to be a reason for it.

I wanted to put her behind me. I'd like to say I hadn't thought of her for twenty-five years, but that's not at all true. No, I've thought about her just about every single day since my buddies and I stumbled upon her cottage on the mountain. About what she said. About what parts came true, and how she knew it all would happen, just like she said.

You're going nowhere with your life, boy.
Best you can hope for is a dead-end job,
pumping gas and cleaning windows.
All your friends will leave you behind
and go on to do big things.
I can see it clearly.
But not you.
You are a failure from a long line of failures.
That's all you'll ever be.
Come back to me when you feel the reaper calling.

Chapter Three

I don't know how I could have forgotten all about the river that separated this part of the forest from the base of the mountains. Back in the day, we had gone quite a way off course to find a crossing, since we were trying to avoid the main road that the logging trucks and hikers took. The only other way we found was the rail bridge.

The rail company once kept the rail corridor trimmed and clear from any overgrowth. When the train still ran through this area, that is. After the printing press and the tractor engine factory skipped out of town for better talent and bigger cities, there were no real exports from Tower Falls to support the rail line. I recalled this as I tripped over one side of the railroad track that jutted up among the twigs and weeds. My chin split open and poured out down my neck. I'll need to trash my white t-shirt after this fine day that I've made for myself.

I followed the rail a mile or so. After a bend, the iron girders of the bridge jutted into my vision. We cut it close crossing that thing back then, but I no longer had to worry about racing a speeding engine. I bet I could do it again if I needed to. If there's one thing I am good at, it's running. Everyone says I am.

Running from my problems.

Running from responsibility.

Running from the law.

Running from anyone who tries to help me or show me love.

Hell, I outran my friends then. I was the first to make it across. Jamie and Berto threw themselves off when they felt the heat of the train. Chubs—Charles—somehow managed to grasp on to one of the girders and hang over the edge. I laughed watching him pull himself up after. Some friend I was. Everyone was miraculously okay in the end.

When my feet reached the last edge of solid ground for the next several hundred yards, I realized the error of my optimism. The trees in the rail corridor weren't the only thing the rail company stopped maintaining. If crossing the bridge on foot was sketchy back then, it was damn near suicidal now. The wooden slats that ran perpendicular under the rails were cracked, rotted, or missing completely. The rails themselves bowed and dipped into nothingness in several parts. The low wooden railings that once ran along either side were now just a distant memory, probably housing fish down in the river below.

I had come this far. Why turn back now?

I took a step onto the right side of the rail track. It seemed stable enough.

Five steps. Ten. Before I knew it, I was almost halfway.

Meow.

I turned too suddenly, trying to face the cats that had come up behind me, and I twisted my ankle. My balance faltered. My foot left the bowing beam of track I had been treading on.

I'm not sure where the strength came from, but I found myself holding on for my hot mess of a life. The splintered timber was somehow holding my weight. My right shoe felt loose as I dangled helplessly over the river far below. I felt a strong temptation to just let myself go. A pull, stronger than gravity. But then something else was keeping me hanging there.

The wedding.

Lizzie.

I had to be there for her. I had to survive this. I managed to support my weight, lift my bloated, middle-aged body back up onto the bridge. Laughter came from somewhere within me as I sprawled across the tracks, but I didn't seem to scare away those damn cats. They were circled all around me like a scene from *Batman Returns*. I got up and followed them the rest of the way across without any more incident.

The track curved and ran alongside the mountain— now towering above me—for a quarter mile or so. I intended to leave the track and cut through the trees to the base of the mountain, but the cats had another idea. They continued to follow the track. They hadn't failed me on the bridge, so I wasn't about to distrust them now. I turned and trailed after them, trying my best to keep up this time.

Chapter Four

The opening of the tunnel wasn't all that narrow. The train had fit through it just fine. It just *felt* a little small, what with the rock-slides that had built up in front of it, and the weeds that grew from those rocks, and the patchwork of spider-webs that kept some little buggers well-fed on tunnel flies. I was pretty sure some of those spiders were crawling around in my sweaty mop of hair. No matter how much I swatted at the webs dangling in front of my face, I couldn't clear it all away.

It got dark in there. *Real* dark. The cats seemed to have no fear, so I knew I'd be okay, but I still couldn't help imagining some mutant freak creature mauling me there in the pitch black. Ain't nobody would come looking for ol' Freddy Goodman in the defunct rail tunnel. Nobody. Lizzie might be the only one to notice I was gone, and her sisters and pals would make sure she forgot all about me in no time at all. Probably hook her up with Jacob Farmer while my corpse rots away in here. Skeleton filled with spiders' nests. Some bum wanders in and takes my skull to his tent to use as an ash tray. Just my luck.

I didn't give up though. I couldn't let myself. I made it out to the other side. Sunlight never felt so good. From there, the cats turned up a steep bit of trail they had made over the years. We climbed up and up. The clouds rolled in before I knew it, and it got damn frigid up there. Those clouds broke open. It poured, and the dirt incline the cats were leading me up turned to mud in no time at all. The first time I slipped, I managed to grab hold of some plants. Just my luck if it was poison ivy. The second time was a doozy. My left pinky got caught in the brambles as I tried to slow my roll down the hill. It swelled up as thick as my thumb but didn't seem broken.

When I finally got to the top, the rainclouds had already moved on. An ancient barbed wire fence was my reward for reaching the crest of that hill. I didn't let that stop me. I had plenty of experience hopping fences like that with only minimal damage.

The rest of the way was quite smooth. I recognized the area from all those years ago. The small pond was still there, the one where we had all fought and swore we'd never hang out again if we survived our little odyssey, but a few minutes later we were all swinging from an old frayed rope and launching ourselves into the water for a swim. Forgiveness was so easy back then. In the years since, someone had replaced that rope with a new one, which was quite weathered now, and even tied a worn-down tire to one end. I was almost tempted to test it out, go for a splash, and wash away all this mud off of me, but that was kids' stuff.

I've got a man's work to do up here.

I knew I was on the last stretch of trail before the old woman's hut.

My fists were clenched. My breathing was coming in heavy grunts, and it wasn't even out of fatigue. Every step closer up that trail brought another ounce of rage to the surface. That old witch had the nerve to live the high life up here, enjoying nature in her little cottage, scaring kids that stumbled into her yard, cursing them for the rest of their lives. Cursing me.

Did her cats know who they were bringing up to their master? Did she send them down to me? Did she know I would follow? I was sure of it. She wanted to curse me yet again. To ruin my happy day. To tell me how I would mess up the remainder of my life, destroy my relationship with Lizzie. And I was going to let her. What power did I have over a witch?

I stopped at the last bend. I remembered the smell of meat cooking in her fireplace that drew us there as kids. It reached our noses down at the pond. She must have known we were there playing, must have heard the splashes and the youthful laughs. Probably watched us from up above, reading each of us, preparing for what she'd say to us.

And she was right about each of us. Me especially.

She was right that I'd flunk out of school. That I'd end up in jail before I could even drink, and that I wouldn't be able to keep away from those iron bars. That I'd stick around in town because I was too incompetent to find a way out. That I'd become my old man. That I'd fail at everything, let down everyone, drive away every person that ever tried loving me.

I was going to show her how right she was. She was waiting for me. I felt it. Deep in my bones, I knew she was waiting for me.

I dropped to my knees as soon as I turned that corner.

Chapter Five

She had the table laid out for us when we arrived. A small chunk of rabbit on each plate, boiled carrots, and stale bread. She even set out little glasses of red wine even though we were twelve-year-old kids. It was a strange, silent meal, but all four of us boys seemed to be under her power, and we were hungry from all the hiking and camping we'd done. Afterwards, she let us poke around her cabin and the yard.

Charles kept eating whatever food was still on the table. Berto picked up an old acoustic guitar with rusted-out strings and made it sound as good as a middle schooler could. Jamie had a few cats crawling all over his lap, letting them lick his hands and cheeks. I stood at the far edge of the yard, not trusting the lady that had just fed us. I was throwing pebbles off the side of the hill that overlooked the forest below and the town beyond.

I spotted another one of those cats climbing up the hillside through some thorny bushes. I don't know why

I did it, even when I knew she was watching, but I picked up a rock the size of my fist and lobbed it down at that cat. It hit him straight in the eye.

"There is nothing good about you, young man," the witch said to me. Then she had us sit next to the fire while she proceeded to tell us our futures. Berto was going to leave town and become a world-class musician. Charles was going to be a chef and open his own restaurant in a big city. Jamie would go on to take care of animals. Turned out she was pretty spot-on with those predictions.

And then she turned to me. She unloaded on me about every way I was going to be a failure. She went on and on about all the evil and low-down shit I'd go on to do. How I would die alone, with nobody to mourn me, loved by no family, friend, or partner. And I sat there, weeping in front of all my friends, taking in every word. They didn't know how to act around me, but they also didn't stand up for me.

Because they knew she was telling the truth. She was a witch, after all. She had seen it all in her tea leaves or her crystal ball or some crazy premonitions or something.

Our friendships faded slowly over the next few years. I finally dropped out during senior year of high school, just like she said I would. They all left town over the first summer I spent in jail, and we never talked again.

She held her power over me all these years, and now here I was, ready to do who knows what.

But I couldn't.

The frame of the cottage was smaller than I remembered. It was just one room, big enough for a single bed, some chairs around a small table, an ancient cooking stove and fire pit, and a couple counters.

All that was left of it was the remnants of a caved-in roof. Crumbling portions of walls otherwise covered in vines. A tree grew right up out of the center.

I stood up and climbed over the rubble to get inside—if it could even be considered as such. The chairs were crushed, the pieces littering the worm-eaten floor. A rat jumped out of the remains of the fire pit and scurried through a hole in the wall. Off in the corner, on the bed, was what was left of that witch.

She had died.

Alone.

Unloved.

Unmourned.

Come back to me when you feel the reaper calling.

I crept over to her side. In death, she looked small. Weak. Human.

"I thought you had power over me. All these years, I let your words—and everyone else's—tell me who I was supposed to be, how I was supposed to fail." The words choked out of me amid ugly sobs. "Looking at you now, I can see how stupid I was to listen to you."

I found the remains of her blankets. I picked them up, shook the dust and rodent droppings off of them, and covered up her bones.

"You were wrong, though. It was you who died with nothing and nobody to care about you. Look at you. All alone up here, rotting away. It's pathetic. You arc pathetic. I'm done being under your power. I'm done living to anyone's expectations. I'm turning it around right now. May you rest in hell, witch."

I turned to find the cats all perched on the crumbled stone walls, watching me with those haunting feline eyes. I don't know what they wanted from me. To stay, perhaps. To be alone up here like their last master, to fail my loved ones, to scare children away, to be a stain on this earth.

"I'm sorry," I said to them, and then I left the witch's domain.

The sun was starting to get lower in the sky, so I didn't waste time on the way down. I reached the parking lot of the hiking trail just as Joey Feldman and his wife were loading up their mountain bikes in the back of their truck.

"Ain't you supposed to be getting hitched right about now, Goodman?" Joey asked. I grunted something, but I was in too much of a hurry to stop for a chat.

"Hop in the back," Stacy Feldman called after me. "We'll take you back to town with us. Lizzie gon' be waiting."

I took her up on the offer and climbed into the bed of the truck. I had a wedding to head to, the bloody mess that I was in my mud-caked work clothes.

After all, Lizzie was waiting, and I was done letting people down.

Direct From the Author

Please visit my website MacheteAndQuill.com, where you'll find signed books, ebooks, and more. Due to the rules of Kindle Unlimited, my ebooks enrolled in that program cannot be sold on my own website. However, the rest of my ebooks as well as signed paperbacks and hardcovers of all my books and stories can be purchased from my website for customers in the US. I like to ship extra goodies such as stickers, coasters, and postcards with all orders. Buying from me directly helps me retain more of the profit, but I truly appreciate purchases made from any retailer you feel most comfortable buying from.

Please also review on Goodreads, Amazon, and Facebook readers groups to get the word out. Finally, please sign up for my newsletter on my site so we can stay in touch. Thank you.

Also by Ryan Hoyt

HORROR AND DARK FICTION

Raventree Hollow

Something evil is feeding off the sins of Raventree Hollow. Shirley Jackson's "The Possibility of Evil" meets Stephen King's *Needful Things* in *Raventree Hollow*, an American gothic horror tale set in the 1950s. A standalone story, it is the first book of the new *A Machete & Quill Horror* line.

We Are Not Alone in the Dark

A high school bully, quarreling friends, and an abusive father are the least of Bryan's worries. When night comes, so do the visitors, and he can't fight back. Who will rescue Bryan if nobody even believes him? A standalone coming-of-age horror novel.

EPIC FANTASY

The Forest of Despair

A heroine's first adventure. A kingdom's last hope. The new female-led epic fantasy series The Pierced Shadow Archive begins here.

The Isle of Abandonment

She once saved a kingdom with her friends. Now she must do it alone. Gemma Calvertson's story continues months after the events of *The Forest of Despair* as she and her friends face their biggest challenges yet.

The Realm Beyond

To help her friends and bring truth to the people of Aepistelle, she must join the ranks of her enemy King Davin and his Royal Mystic Committee. Gemma Calvertson's story ends here.

The Witch of Ferathan

An alluring stranger. A trail of destruction. Will Ferathan survive her charm? *The Witch of Ferathan*, a Pierced Shadow Archive novella, is set seventy years before the events of *The Forest of Despair* and can be read as a standalone story.

About the Author

Ryan Hoyt's tales of fantasy and horror arise from the depths of all the books and movies his parents allowed him to consume as a child in the San Francisco Bay Area. Ryan currently resides near Sacramento, CA. His wife Marsha serves as his biggest supporter, while his two daughters secure their roles as his toughest critics. He also hosted The Machete and Quill Podcast, exploring the world of his fantasy series The Pierced Shadow Archive. Outside of writing, Ryan works in internet trust and safety, where the real horrors stem from.